"Hello, Sydn____ whispered.

"You're the last person on earth I ever expected to see again in this lifetime…let alone here," she began.

"It's a long story." His voice rasped. "I came as soon as I could."

She stared at him in utter bewilderment. "What do you mean?"

He cocked his dark, attractive head. "The day you left town you asked me if I would leave with you. At the time, I couldn't give you an answer."

That moment had been so excruciating she experienced physical pain all over again remembering it. Anger consumed her.

"So now you've decided you *can*?" she mocked in raw agony, remembering the kiss he'd given her that had said "goodbye forever."

Rebecca Winters, whose family of four children has now swelled to include three beautiful grandchildren, lives in Salt Lake City, Utah, in the land of the Rocky Mountains. With canyons and high Alpine meadows full of wildflowers, she never runs out of places to explore. They, plus her favourite vacation spots in Europe, often end up as backgrounds for her Tender Romance™ novels, because writing is her passion, along with her family and church. Rebecca loves to hear from her readers. If you wish to e-mail her, please visit her website at: www.rebeccawinters.com

Recent titles by the same author:

HUSBAND BY REQUEST
THEIR NEW-FOUND FAMILY
FATHER BY CHOICE

MEANT-TO-BE MARRIAGE

BY
REBECCA WINTERS

MILLS & BOON®

First published in Great Britain 2006
Harlequin Mills & Boon Limited,
Eton House, 18-24 Paradise Road, Richmond, Surrey TW9 1SR

© Rebecca Winters 2006

ISBN 0 263 84890 6

Set in Times Roman 12¼ on 14¾ pt.
02-0406-45541

Printed and bound in Spain
by Litografia Rosés, S.A., Barcelona

CHAPTER ONE

"I ABSOLUTELY REFUSE to let the memory of a priest ruin my entire life! Since he'll always be forbidden to me, let this be the end of my pain."

So saying, Sydney tossed her sheaf of roses into the water and watched the waves carry it out to sea. Turning swiftly away, she hurried up the sandy path to the backyard of the Brysons' fabulous San Diego home.

Now that the honeymooners had gone, the grounds overlooking the Pacific Ocean had emptied of wedding guests. Except for the maids who were cleaning up, Sydney found herself alone.

Earlier, she and the wedding party had greeted a crowd of several hundred who'd congregated here after the Friday afternoon church service.

The prominent Bryson family had spared no expense for their only daughter's nuptials.

Ranger Gilly Bryson King had been claimed as the bride of Dr. Alex Latimer, the legendary ranger in charge of the Volcano Observatory at Yellowstone Park.

Like the handsome prince and the beautiful princess in a fairy tale, the radiant couple in a black tuxedo and flowing white wedding dress had stood a little distance off with the pounding surf below providing the breathtaking backdrop.

Being the maid of honor, Sydney had wanted to look her best for her dear friend. As a result, she'd taken particular care to find the right pink-frost lipstick to highlight the mold of her wide, curving mouth. A little blusher on her cheek-bones, the kind only a close friend like Gilly would say made her such a classic beauty, and she'd been ready to face guests.

Among them were a large group of rangers from Yellowstone and Teton Parks who'd flown down for the wedding, which had been a huge affair. Somehow Sydney had been able to get through the festivities without any of her former colleagues being the wiser concerning her latest plans.

Two weeks earlier, Chief Ranger Archer had reluctantly accepted her resignation as a park ranger. Per her wishes, he'd promised to keep quiet about it until she'd left the Park for good.

Sydney had already vacated her cabin, and had moved into a furnished apartment in Gardiner, Montana, before coming to the wedding. No one but the chief knew she'd be teaching school there for the next year. That was the way she wanted it. Otherwise people would ask questions she wasn't ready to answer.

Except for Gilly, her former co-workers wouldn't understand that her unexpected career change had been made out of a desperate need for self-preservation. It seemed that being a ranger hadn't brought the forgetfulness she'd craved.

After a quick visit to her parents in Bismarck, she would fly to Gardiner to begin her new life. Hopefully her teaching duties would force her not to dwell on a love that was never meant to be. Otherwise her whole future was destined to be an eternal punishment.

Once more she looked out at the sea. The late August sun was about to set. Its rays created a golden nimbus that gilded her jaw-length blond curls. Even without a breeze, they had a tendency to look a little windswept due to the expertise of a clever stylist.

As her gaze watched the fiery orange ball drop into the ocean and disappear, she noticed to her dismay that the undercurrent had brought her brilliant pink flowers back to shore. Their battered heads lay strewn across the sand, a frightening omen.

Normally the tiny flecks in her irises took on the color of most any outfit she chose to wear, like the hyacinth tone of her lace-trimmed suit. Once upon a time the man who was out of reach to her forever—the man she shouldn't be thinking about now—the man who'd ruined her for all other men in existence—had told her he counted half the hues of the spectrum in them ranging from gray-green to lavender-blue.

Right now her eyes were haunted and resembled a dark sky seconds before a tornado touched down. Sydney let out a frightened cry and dashed inside the house to change and pack for her early flight to Bismarck in the morning.

It was close to midnight when Jarod Kendall pulled the car into the driveway of the rectory in Cannon, North Dakota. After the grueling session at church headquarters in Bismarck, followed by the hour's drive home, Jarod didn't know how another priest in his situation would be feeling right now.

He couldn't speak for anyone else. All he knew was relief that the struggle was finally over.

"Father?" Rick's voice called to him from the bottom of the staircase after he'd let himself in the house.

"I didn't realize you were still awake."

"Welcome back. Kay's asleep. I wanted to clear a few things with you before we leave for church in the morning. It'll only take a moment, but if you're too—"

His deacon stopped talking midsentence. He'd drawn close enough to see that Jarod was wearing a man's regular business suit and tie. There was nothing about him to remind anyone even remotely that he'd once worn priestly robes.

Jarod had hoped to spare Rick the shock tonight, but since he was still up, maybe it was better this way. To have waited until morning would have made it harder on Rick, who'd be expected to carry on as if nothing was wrong. At least this way he'd have the rest of the night to absorb it and talk it over with Kay.

No matter how torn Jarod was to have left the priesthood, the luxury to be able to turn to your wife, whether in passion or the need for comfort, was something he craved.

"Come in my study, Rick. I have some news for you."

Like a sleepwalker, Rick followed him inside.

"Sit down," Jarod invited before taking his own seat behind the desk.

The other man sank into the leather chair, looking pale. "When you went on vacation this last week, Kay and I wondered if something was wrong. We thought you might be ill and didn't want anyone to know."

"I *have* been ill, Rick. *So* ill, in fact, that two months ago, I took the final step to get well and laid my case before the church. As of today, I'm no longer Father Kendall."

A gasp from the other man resounded in the study.

"Tomorrow, Father Lane will be officiating as the parochial vicar until a new priest has been announced."

Rick's eyes filled with tears. "Why?"

"Before you and Kay moved here, I fell in love with a woman named Sydney Taylor who left over fifteen months ago. She was a high school English teacher who encouraged one of her students to get professional counseling through the church.

"Brenda Halverson was sixteen, and had just found out she was going to have a baby. Her first instinct was to end her unwanted pregnancy. Since she was terrified to tell her parents, she wrote about it in the daily journal she kept for Sydney's English class.

"From the moment I met Sydney, who accompanied the girl to her first session with me, my life has been conflicted. At Brenda's insistence, Sydney came to all the sessions with her, but the truth is, we couldn't stay away from each other.

"Sometimes I've noticed you watching me with concern. No doubt you were witnessing my struggle to try to forget her. A few months ago I made inquiries and found out she's still single.

"Before you attempt to dissuade me from the decision I've already made, let me assure you I've had fifteen months to search my soul for what is right for me. Fifteen months to consider what I'd be giving up. Fifteen months to realize that once I left, there'd be no going back.

"I'm not like some of the parishioners who've come to me because they've been suffering in a bad marriage and want a divorce. I love the Church. It goes without saying I love my life in it. It tears me apart to have to make a choice, but I love Sydney too much. Since I can't have both, I've left the priesthood to go after her.

"You have no idea how I envy you and Kay. As far as I'm concerned, seeing you together enjoying all the blessings of marriage while you serve the Church has to be the epitome of joy in this life."

Jarod noticed his friend's shoulders shaking in silent grief.

"The question of married clergy has always been out there, Rick. I don't know why I haven't been able to put her out of my mind and heart. We've had no contact in all that time. Absolutely nothing. And yet…I'm on fire for her," he whispered fiercely.

Rick's head reared. "Then she doesn't know what you've done—"

"No. But I'm convinced she hasn't married because she hasn't been able to put me out of her mind, either. Yet I could hardly go to her as an ordained priest.

"When I face her, it has to be as a free man. She has to see me as an ordinary male before her mind will allow her to peel away the layers of Father Kendall from her consciousness."

"I can understand that," he said at last. "When your petition is put through to the Vatican, will they grant you laicization?"

"Probably not. Leaving the priesthood without permission is something I'm going to have to live with. But as I've discovered, living without Sydney would mean I'd only half exist from here on out, which isn't fair to the parish. That's not the life I want to live."

"Heaven knows I don't blame you, Jarod. I thought I wanted to become a priest…until I met Kay."

"Thank you for your honesty, Rick. But not many others will be as understanding. You think I don't realize how many people I'll be letting down, who've grown to depend on me? The money the Church spent on my training? The effect my leaving will have on the other priests in the diocese when they learn that Father Kendall has left the priesthood?"

"But not the Church!" Rick's voice rang out.

"No. Never that."

Rick let out a pained sigh. "You're so certain she still feels the same way?"

"Deep down I believe she does, yes."

"What if she's changed?"

"That's a risk I have to take."

"Have you considered she might turn you down?"

"It's a real possibility. But no matter her circumstances, I have to go to her unencumbered if I expect her to listen to me."

"And if she doesn't, you'll have given up all you achieved in the hope that she still loves you."

"Yes."

By this time Rick was on his feet. He stared hard at Jarod. "Did you sleep with her?"

"No. We held each other for a brief moment when she told me she was leaving, but we didn't do anything but ache for each other."

A bewildered look crossed over his face. "Then—"

"It doesn't matter, Rick. There was this feeling between us that transcends my ability to put into words. Fifteen months are gone. I'm going to be thirty-eight on my next birthday. Every minute that passes is taking something away from us we can't get back."

"You won't be able to marry in the Church."

"I know."

"Is she devout?"

"She's not Catholic."

"What?"

"She was baptized in the Lutheran church, but hasn't attended any church in years."

"Forgive me, Father, but in your case that might help."

A strange sound escaped Jarod's throat. "I'm not a priest anymore, Rick."

"You are to me."

"Besides the Bishop at the diocese, you've been my closest friend. So I'm going to remind you there's no magic solution here. It would require turning back the clock and arranging for Sydney to teach at a school anywhere in North Dakota but Cannon so we wouldn't have met."

"Kay's going to take this hard. She thinks of you as the perfect priest."

Jarod frowned. "That's the trouble with perfection. There is no such thing."

"In her heart she'll be rooting for you, Jarod."

"I know that. To help her out, I'll be gone long before she wakes up in the morning. It'll make it easier for everyone. Father Lane will stay here for the interim to oversee the affairs of the parish. He'll tell everyone I've gone on retreat. By the time the new priest is announced, it'll be a smooth transition."

"How will you live?"

Rick's question jerked Jarod out of his reverie.

"I've made tentative arrangements to do counseling in Gardiner, Montana. It's a town five miles from Yellowstone Park. That way when Sydney and I are married, she can continue to be a park ranger if that's what she wants to do."

"She's a ranger?"

"Yes."

"And she doesn't know you're coming?"

"No." His hands formed into fists. "What I need is the element of surprise. No matter what she says to my face, I'll be able to read the truth of her initial feelings in her eyes."

"She might faint on you. Have you thought of that?"

"I don't think she's the type."

"I would think any woman was the type if she were suddenly confronted by the man she'd once known as Father Kendall." His Adam's apple bobbed. "You're the most courageous man I've ever known."

"Courageous—" Jarod blurted incredulously.

"Yes. For knowing your heart well enough to face yourself and God with the absolute conviction you're doing the right thing."

He shook his head. "You're one in a million, Rick. But being sure of my decision doesn't take away the pain of leaving the life I've loved all these years. It's tearing me apart," he confessed.

"It tears me up, too. I'm going to miss you."

"The feeling's mutual." The two men stared solemnly at each other before Jarod said, "It's past time for bed. You're going to have a full day tomorrow helping Father Lane get oriented."

"I'm going upstairs, but promise me something first."

"For you, anything."

"Stay in touch."

"Of course."

Rick paused in the doorway. "I've loved and revered Father Kendall. That hasn't changed because he has set off on a new path. If there's to be a wedding in the future, Kay and I would come in an instant. I would consider it an honor to stand up for you if you want me there."

Jarod's eyes smarted as he studied his friend. "It's not a case of if, but *when*."

* * *

Sydney had arranged for a rental car ahead of time. When she arrived in Bismarck, she had every intention of driving straight to her parents' home beyond the city limits.

But after leaving the airport, the road sign for Cannon loomed up on her right. Only forty-five miles away and she could satisfy her craving to see *him* again at Mass. It began at ten. She still had enough time to make it. He'd never know she was there if she stayed at the back of the church.

Just a few minutes to last the rest of her life…

Despising herself for giving in to her weakness, yet helpless to do anything else, she pushed caution aside and headed west. She pressed on the accelerator, unconcerned that a highway patrol car would probably pull her over at this speed.

She didn't care. Her heart was beating so wildly, she needed the physical release. Right now nothing mattered but to feast her eyes on him again.

Except for a few small housing developments that had sprung up in the last year, Cannon hadn't changed a great deal. If it had, she wouldn't have noticed anyway. All her attention was riveted to the parish church at the end of Jefferson Street.

Sydney had worn a blue blouse and khaki skirt on the plane. Her outfit was dressy enough to fit in with the other women walking up the steps to enter.

After parking the car, she waited outside the doors until it was almost ten on the dot, then joined a group of people and followed them inside. They would provide enough cover for her to slip inside the last pew.

The people who preceded her had the same idea, so she sat down next to them, keeping her head bowed. But it came up when she heard a different male voice lead the mass.

An older priest was conducting.

Where was Father Kendall?

Crushed with pain and disappointment, Sydney had no choice but to sit there until the mass ended. The second it was over she stole out of the church.

By the time she reached the car, an older woman was getting in the one next to her. She nodded to Sydney, who couldn't prevent herself from asking, "Do you happen to know why Father Kendall wasn't there today?"

"Someone said he was ill."

The news devastated Sydney. "That's too bad."

"I agree. There's no one like him."

No. No one…

She flashed the woman a forced smile. "Have a lovely day."

In the next instant, Sydney climbed in the car and drove off, afraid the other woman might want to prolong the conversation. She couldn't let that happen.

He was ill?

How ill?

It she called his office, he would eventually see her caller ID and know she hadn't had the discipline to leave him alone after all.

"You're out of your mind, Sydney Taylor!"

With tears gushing down her cheeks, she drove back to Bismarck faster than ever. En route she phoned her parents and told them her rental car had suffered a flat tire, which was the reason she'd been detained.

No one could ever know what she'd done. Never, never again would she waste time dwelling on Father Kendall. This was the end, the absolute end of her fixation on him. As of this second, *IT WAS FINISHED*!

Two hours later she followed her father through the back door of the house into the kitchen.

After riding horses with him for a little while, she needed a shower.

"Lunch is ready," her mother announced.

"I'll be with you in five minutes," Sydney promised.

She made it back to the table in four, wearing a clean pair of jeans and a blouse. The only difference between her outfit and her parents' was that her top wasn't plaid.

"Pot roast. My favorite. Thanks, Mom."

Old customs died hard on the plains of North Dakota. Sydney's grandparents and great-grandparents had always served the big meal at midday. Her parents were no different. Beef was usually on the menu.

"What do you think of the North Forty now?" Her mother's question jerked Sydney from her perilous thoughts. The disastrous detour to Cannon had left her shaken and filled with more questions. What if Jarod was seriously ill? She couldn't bear it if that were true.

"I noticed you've gotten rid of a lot of the leafy spurge since June," Sydney murmured before taking another bite of corn on the cob.

Her mother smiled. "Your father decided to try those beetles instead of spraying."

"That was a smart move, Dad."

"They haven't gotten rid of all of the weeds, but they've reduced a fair amount. It didn't cost me as much."

He reached for another helping of roast. "That fellow from the fish and game department knew what he was talking about."

"I'm glad you listened to him."

Her mother passed her the bowl of salad. "After we eat, Lydia wants us to come over for dessert."

"Sounds good." It had been a while since Sydney had seen her aunt and uncle. "How's Jenny?" Her cousin was about ready to have her first baby. Sydney had bought her a present while she'd been in California.

"Blossoming."

"Have they thought of a name yet?"

"Joe." Her father said with a smile.

Sydney nodded. "Can't go wrong with a name like that." Jenny's husband was named Joe. Obviously she'd gone along with the decision. Whatever Joe wanted was fine with her. They had a good marriage. So did Sydney's parents.

On the whole, her mother went along with her dad, but there'd been moments in the past when she'd put her foot down. Very few of them however.

"Did I tell you our ladies group gave Jenny a new car seat and a stroller at her baby shower?"

"That's nice, Mom."

"Some of them are still working on a quilt for her."

"What a lucky baby."

While her parents enjoyed a second cup of coffee, Sydney got up and started clearing the table.

Her mother brought their empty coffee mugs to the sink. "Someday you'll be married and have a husband and children of your own, too."

Sydney had to tamp down her frustration. After taking several deep breaths, she swung around. "Maybe I won't, Mom. Don't count on it."

Don't count on my ever falling in love with anyone else.

Her father joined them at the sink. "Tell us what happened with that fellow Chip from Idaho. We thought he was the one."

"I was never in love with him. That's why it didn't work."

"All along there's been someone else, hasn't there?"

She couldn't lie to her parents. "Yes."

"Is he still in Cannon?" her mother questioned.

Sydney's heart plunged to the floor. Her emotions were in too much chaos after driving there. Anything that involved Father Kendall made her almost physically ill. That's how she felt right now. Especially not knowing how serious his condition was.

How many more years had to pass before the mere thought of him held no power over her? What if his illness was fatal?

Dear God.

"Honey?"

Sydney bowed her head. "Can we please change the subject?"

"You'll feel better if you talk about it," her father persisted. "Until you started teaching in Cannon, you were our happy girl."

Her mother eyed her with concern. "Since you can't discuss it with us, I think you ought to call Pastor Gregson and have a chat with him while you're here."

Sydney let out a frustrated cry. "I'm twenty-six, Mom, hardly a little girl anymore. Pastor Gregson is a stranger to me. In any event, he'd be the last person to understand." Sydney could just imagine their conversation.

I'm in love with a priest, Pastor Gregson.

Then you must do everything to put that devil out of your mind, Sydney.

"Now, Sydney—"

"You know how I feel about church." As far as Sydney was concerned, organized religion seemed to cause a lot more pain than it alleviated. But for it, she and Father Kendall—

No! She'd promised herself she wouldn't go there.

Taking another deep breath, she turned to her mother. "I realize church helps you two deal with the crises in your lives. That's fine. But I have to handle my problems in my own way."

"The pastor has a wonderful reputation." Her father kept it up.

Once her parents dug in their heels, that was it. The church community was their answer for everything.

"If I feel the need for help, I'll arrange to see a psychiatrist."

Sydney had just said the wrong thing again. Her parents didn't believe in psychiatry.

"Is this man already married?"

Yes, he's married. But not in the way you mean.

"No!" Sydney cried in agony. "Now if you'll excuse me, I'll change into something dressier to wear over to Aunt Lydia's."

Before driving into Yellowstone National Park from the North Entrance at Gardiner, Jarod bought a map at a convenience store and ate breakfast in the rental car while he studied it.

His eye traced the 140-mile Grand Loop that formed a figure eight through the Park. From here he could travel south to Madison, then Old Faithful, West Thumb, Fishing Bridge, Tower Falls, Mammoth and the Norris Geyser area.

There were roads leading to other portions of the Park, too. His plan was to look around at each major stopping-off point in the hope of spotting Sydney on the job. He preferred not to query anyone about her. They might alert her that someone was asking questions.

If she was anywhere around, her gilt hair would attract his attention. Whether in her ranger uniform or not, with her long legs and slender curves, she'd be impossible to miss. In the event he had no success, then he'd be forced to make inquiries.

After living at an elevation of 800 feet in Cannon for the last ten years, Jarod could blame his accelerated heart rate on the six-thousand-foot change which made the air thinner. But he knew his vital organ was getting the greatest portion of its workout for an entirely different reason.

Exhilarated in a way he hadn't been in ages because he knew this was Sydney's world, Jarod couldn't help but contrast the beautiful subalpine terrain dotted with lodgepole pines and spruce trees to the windswept plains along the Cannonball River.

The dry heat today might be in the eighties, but it didn't wilt him. As soon as the fast-moving cumulus clouds covered the sun, he felt an immediate drop in temperature.

With each curve in the road he noticed places where forest fires had burned patches of vegetation. Remarkably he could see flowers sprouting from those blackened areas, evidence of new life. *New life.*

His hands tightened on the wheel.

Like the other tourists, he kept an eye out for bison and moose. The Saturday traffic moved slowly. At this rate it would take all day to make a superficial sweep of the Park in his effort to locate her.

By the time he'd reached the Upper Geyser Basin, his patience had worn thin. It shouldn't have surprised him that the Old Faithful area looked like a gigantic parking lot. End-of-summer vacationers had gathered to watch the famous geyser blow.

According to the brochure he'd been given when he'd paid his entry fee, each eruption lasted a different length of time and went off in intervals from thirty to a hundred and twenty minutes. Judging by the mass of people seated on the benches and standing around, a new eruption was imminent.

Once he'd found a place to park, he looped his powerful binoculars around his neck and got out of the car. Everyone had their cameras trained on the scene. While serious photographers set up their tripods in the hope of capturing something unusual and spectacular on film, Jarod started walking around with a different target in mind.

Putting the lens to his eyes, he swept the sea of tourists. So far he'd only picked out a handful of male rangers in uniform, one of whom was speaking to the huge crowd assembled. Convinced Sydney wasn't on duty here, Jarod walked the short distance to the Old Faithful Visitors Center.

Besides a sales outlet, he discovered an auditorium full of at least a hundred people where another male ranger was narrating a film. He saw a couple of others walking around, talking to tourists.

As he turned to leave, he caught sight of a display in one of the alcoves manned by a teenager. There was a banner hanging above her head. Help Build A New Old Faithful Visitor Center.

He moved closer to the winsome brunette and read the tag on her khaki blouse. Cindy Lewis, Junior Park Ranger.

She smiled at him. "Would you like to know why we need a new facility?"

If she could help him find Sydney, Jarod decided he would be happy to hear anything she had to tell him. It was a long shot, but worth his time.

"That's why I stopped."

Her smile broadened. "The need for information, orientation and educational services isn't being met by the existing visitor center. As you can see, this building is too small to accommodate even a small percentage of the people visiting the area.

"There are no interpretive exhibits and the auditorium lacks sufficient seating for the numbers of visitors wanting to see films. That's why the Yellowstone Park Foundation is committed to raising the funds to build a new facility.

"It represents the best opportunity for public-spirited individuals like yourself to join with the National Park Service in building a new, world-class visitor center. There'll be permanent exhibits to help people understand and appreciate the rarest hydrothermal resources on earth today.

"If you're interested in learning more, please take this brochure and read it. Any contribution would be greatly appreciated."

Jarod pulled some money from his wallet and put it in the attached envelope before handing it back to her. "This is for your excellent presentation."

"Thanks!"

"You're welcome. Are there more junior rangers like you around?"

"Yes. We're situated throughout the Park to help educate people, but after the Labor Day weekend we'll have to go back to school."

"It sounds like a very commendable program. Are you planning to become a National Park Ranger after college?"

"Yes."

"I once knew a woman who I understand became a park ranger here."

"I'm friends with all the rangers. What's her name?"

The blood pounded in his ears. "Sydney Taylor."

The girl blinked. "Ranger Taylor has been the head of the teenage junior ranger program all summer! She's the best."

Jarod's adrenaline surged. "Are we speaking of the same person? She used to be a school-teacher at Cannonball High in North Dakota."

"Yes! She said she taught English there for a year before she came here."

"I knew her quite well. What a coincidence that you've been working with her," he murmured. "Do you have any idea where she is right now?"

The girl nodded. "California. Her best friend, Ranger King, just got married. Sydney will be back on Monday."

Frustrated that she wasn't here, he was forced to suppress his fierce disappointment. He needed to come face-to-face with the one woman in the world who'd become necessary to his existence.

"I'd like to leave a note for her. Do you know where she lives?"

"Sure. It's across the parking area, cabin five."

"Thank you, Cindy." He shook her hand. "It's been a pleasure to meet you."

He walked off before she had the presence of mind to ask his name. Within a few minutes he found his car and drove over to the cluster of cabins in the distance.

So much for the element of surprise.

After penning a message, Jarod left the folded paper inside the front door screen where she would see it when she returned from California.

Once inside the car, he started the motor and took off, pressing on the accelerator as he headed back to Gardiner. By tomorrow night he expected her to call him on his cell phone.

Yet he couldn't silence the niggling voice

inside his head asking questions he refused to contemplate.

What if she doesn't respond?

What if she doesn't want anything to do with you?

CHAPTER TWO

THE HARDEST PART about teaching school was enduring the first three days of teachers' meetings before you actually got to meet your students.

At seven-thirty Monday evening, an exhausted Sydney hurried out of Elkhorn High School to her car. Following the day's meetings, the PTA had served dinner in the cafeteria. Tomorrow she would have to come early to start decorating her room before back-to-school night on Wednesday.

Two blocks away she turned into the drive of her eight-plex apartment building and parked her Jeep in one of the covered stalls. What she needed right now was a shower, then bed.

Before reaching the door of her ground-floor unit, she sensed she wasn't alone and assumed it was one of the other tenants coming home, too. Then she heard a man call to her in a low, compelling voice.

The urgent way he said her name conjured memories that made the hairs stand on the back of her neck.

No…

It couldn't be…

It just couldn't…

Still disbelieving, Sydney turned around slowly, convinced the fatigue of the day had taken unprecedented liberties with her imagination.

In the growing darkness she saw the silhouette of a tall, solidly built man. At first glance she thought he bore a resemblance to the man whose memory had been her nemesis. But two things stood out that made her decide she was mistaken, that she was looking at a stranger.

For one thing he was wearing a tan suit with a tie. The man she'd once known would never be dressed in such clothes.

For another, this man with his jet-black hair and brows was *beardless*.

Through her lashes she studied the unfamiliar lines of a strong chin and jaw with their five o'clock shadow. He possessed a potently male mouth hinting at an aggression that made her swallow hard.

"*Sydney*—" he whispered, reading her confusion correctly.

The deep cadence of his voice permeated to the core of her being. Like a matching fingerprint, there was no mistaking who he was this time. The reality of his presence sent her into shock. She fell against the door helplessly.

He started to move toward her.

"No—don't touch me!" she begged. But her protest went ignored as the flesh-and-blood man placed his hands on her upper arms to steady her. She felt their heat as if she'd pressed up against a furnace.

"I'll let you go when you're able to walk without help."

Sydney's head fell back on the graceful column of her neck. Her heart pounded in her ears.

"Come on. Let's get you inside." He took the keys from her nerveless fingers and opened the door.

Convinced she was hallucinating, she started to feel light-headed. Her legs refused to obey her.

The next moment became a blur. With effortless masculine strength, he picked her up in his arms and carried her into the dimly lit living room. After laying her on the couch, he disappeared.

A minute later he returned with a glass of water. Hunkering down next to her, he put it to her lips. His other hand slid beneath the gold satin of her hair to prop her head.

"Drink as much as you can. It'll help."

Though her head was spinning, she did his bidding before handing the empty glass back to him. He put it on the coffee table.

Between his silky black lashes, the eyes she remembered burned like hot green coals. Combined with the male beauty of his features, he was so impossibly handsome, she groaned in reaction.

When it became clear he really was here in person, her strength began to return and she carefully sat up. Another minute and she was able to get to her feet, desperate to disguise the fact that she'd been staring at him with an intense hunger he couldn't have helped but notice.

He stood a little distance apart from her with his hands on his hips, reminding her once again what an incredible-looking man he was.

Back in Cannon, the beard had made him

seem more untouchable and intimidating. Without it, he…

She rubbed her arms as if she were freezing to death. In truth she was burning up inside with so many emotions, she couldn't name them all. But topping the list was rage and anger for his coming here to enlarge the wound that had never healed.

"I have to admit you're the last person on earth I ever expected to see again in this life-time…let alone here," she began.

Jarod's eyes glittered. "Evidently you didn't get my note."

Sydney struggled to catch her breath. "What note?"

"The one I left inside the front door screen of your cabin at Old Faithful."

She put a hand to her throat. "When did you do that?"

"Saturday."

Saturday she'd been told he was ill, yet seeing him she realized he'd never looked healthier.

"I—I'd already moved out and was at my parents'."

I had the greatest breakdown of my life by driving over to Cannon to see you. But you weren't there, and you're not ill. What's going on?

He grimaced. "When I didn't hear from you all day today, I had a talk with Chief Ranger Archer. He told me you'd accepted a teaching job here, so I called around until I found you."

Shock still held her in its grip. "I—I can't imagine how you even knew I was a ranger."

"It's a long story," his voice rasped. "I came as soon as I could."

She stared at him in utter bewilderment. "What do you mean?"

He cocked his dark, attractive head. "The day you left Cannon you said, 'I can't stay, and you can't come, can you?' At the time, I couldn't give you an answer."

That moment had been so excruciating, she experienced physical pain all over again re-membering it. For him to be so inhuman as to remind her of it—

Anger consumed her.

"So now you've decided you *can*?" she mocked in raw agony, remembering the kiss he'd given her that had said "goodbye forever."

She backed away from him. "If you thought it would be safe to take a vacation from the Lord with *me*, then you never knew me, and I never knew you." Her pain resounded off the walls of the living room. "Find someone else with whom you can indulge your needs before returning to your unsuspecting flock, *Father Kendall*."

His features hardened like a block of chiseled granite. He made no move to go. "My name is Jarod. I'd like to hear you say it."

She shook her head. "You mean you want me to use it while you're away from Cannon and no one can see us?"

But even as she questioned his motives, she had to inspect her own motives that had propelled her to Cannon two days ago.

He gazed at her for a troubling moment. "You obviously need more time to absorb the fact I'm really here."

"Time?" she bit out. "I admit there was a time when even though I knew it was impossible, the foolish part of me needed to hear you tell me you loved me so much, you would give up your vocation for me.

"That's how naive, stupid, lovestruck and pathetic I once was. But after fifteen months, that person no longer exists.

"*You're* the delusional one if you think you can just show up here without your collar and expect me to fall at your feet because you've got a little time on your hands away from everyone who knows you."

The second the words left her lips, she realized how foolish that sounded. Minutes ago she'd almost fainted at the sight of him. In the next breath she cried, "I have no interest in you or your life!"

What a hypocrite she was.

"Please go!"

"I've missed you, too, Sydney. Try to get some sleep. I'll see you tomorrow," was all he said before he disappeared from her apartment.

Like someone who'd survived a battle and was the only one left alive, she stood there weaving in dazed shock.

When she'd done everything in her power to forget him, how could he be so cruel as to show up now after all this time had passed?

He'd known why she'd left Cannon. One of them had to leave, and it certainly wouldn't have been the priest who'd dedicated his life to God and the parish!

Where was the sensitivity she'd seen in him during those months of counseling he'd given one of her students?

After those first few visits to his office with

Brenda Halverson who was pregnant and afraid to tell her Catholic parents the truth, Sydney should have obeyed her instincts and quit her job. Any lie to break her teaching contract would have been worth it to get far away from *him.*

But her attraction to him had been so powerful, she couldn't bear the thought of not seeing him again. The visits to his office with Brenda while he counseled her were all that had kept Sydney going that year.

He came to the high school activities where Brenda and other students in the parish were involved. She would talk to him then. Sometimes they saw each other on the street in passing and would stop to chat for a little while. Other times she attended Mass with Brenda where she could legitimately feast her eyes on him. Those were the moments she'd lived for. But it was no life!

On the morning she left Cannon, she'd stopped by his office to say goodbye. Another grave mistake. One she would always regret.

He had no indication of what was coming. When she told him she was on her way out of town for good, he got up from the chair and walked over to the closed door where she was standing. He looked physically hurt.

Inside she rejoiced at the anguish that had suddenly darkened his beautiful eyes. For once the facade had slipped, allowing her to see the full extent of his emotions. They told her he was in great pain, too.

She *wanted* him to be in pain. It was selfish of her, but she couldn't help it.

"You're really leaving?" he whispered. His voice sounded thick, gravelly.

"As soon as I walk out of this office. My bags are packed in the car."

"*Sydney*—"

The way he said her name ripped her insides apart.

"I can't stay." Her voice trembled. "You can't come with me. Can you?"

Their gazes clung for an infinity of time.

A heavy silence filled the room. It lasted so long she thought he was getting ready to tell her the one thing she needed to hear that would keep her from going anywhere.

Instead, he pulled her into his arms and kissed her mouth. It gave her a taste of all the things they would never share. Not each other's bodies, not each other's thoughts, hearts or souls, not each other's hopes, dreams, not their joy or laughter, not their children.

Nothing…

When the message was received, she tore her lips from his and ran from his arms, from his office, from the tiny town she would never see again. She'd been running ever since.

Except for her slip on Saturday when all she'd wanted to do was look at him for a little while unobserved, she'd stayed away.

How was it possible he'd traced her here?

Why dredge up the most agonizing experience of her life?

Had it hurt his pride that since their parting she hadn't come crawling back to him like a beggar? In order to satisfy his ego, had he planned this side trip to Yellowstone to provoke her into a clandestine relationship with him?

It wasn't going to happen!

Maybe he got his jollies from imagining there was a woman out there who longed for him. Even if he'd only been able to get as far as his thoughts where Sydney was concerned, did that mean he had no conscience?

Could he honestly go back to his world without it disturbing the tenor of his existence?

She'd bet her life his colleagues in the diocese didn't know where he was, or what he was trying to do, let alone why…

Thank heaven they didn't know what Sydney had been doing on Saturday.

He had to know that coming to Yellowstone was an unconscionable act on his part. When he returned to Cannon, would he confess what he'd done?

A priest on the up and up probably would. But Father Jarod Kendall would no doubt consider himself exempt from confession because he hadn't yet committed an overt act against the commandments.

It took two, and *she* hadn't been available after all.

Did he truly believe she would welcome any crumbs he threw her way because she was so beguiled by him she couldn't help herself?

An icy smile broke out on her lips. She walked over to the door and locked it. For once *he* would learn what it was like to have the door eternally closed to him. Let him rail against it till he was bloodied.

Damn you forever, Father Kendall.

Shaking from emotions she had no idea how

to control, she started to undress so she could shower. When her cell phone rang, she jumped.

Had he managed to get her number from Chief Archer, too? She plucked the phone from her purse and clicked on.

"Hello," she said in a terse tone.

"Sydney?" Cindy Lewis questioned tentatively.

It wasn't Father Kendall on the other end after all. Furious at herself because she felt a gush of disappointment, Sydney disciplined herself to calm down. "Hi, Cindy."

"You sound odd. Are you okay?"

She took deep breaths. "Yes. I just came in to get ready for bed."

"How was the wedding?"

"Fabulous. Jamal Carter told me specifically to say hello to *you* when I talked to you next."

"He did?" she cried excitedly.

"Yes. His mom and sister came all the way from Indianapolis with him for the wedding. They're as nice as Jamal. I found out Alex and Gilly have invited him to live with them next summer and work in the Park."

"You're kidding—"

"Nope. I've got pictures of him in his tuxedo. I'm going to have double prints made up so you can have your own set. He looked even better in the tux than in his junior ranger uniform."

"Jamal's cute."

"He's very cute." Sydney smoothed the hair off her forehead. "Listen, Cindy—I've got some things I have to do right now. If you don't mind, I'll call you next weekend so we can talk longer."

"I'd love that! But before you hang up, I wanted to tell you that some man came to the Park on Saturday looking for you."

"What man?" Sydney played dumb, trying to stifle the moan that escaped.

"He left the visitors center before I could ask his name, but he said he knew you back in Cannon when you were a teacher."

"Really?"

"Yeah. He made a thousand dollar donation to the new visitor center fund."

Sydney almost dropped the phone. Where did a priest with a low income get that kind of money? Why would he do such a thing? "That was incredibly generous of him. Was he there with his family?"

"I don't know. When he walked over to the display, he was alone. He was more gorgeous than a movie star."

Sydney had thought the same thing the first time she'd laid eyes on Jarod.

"Does that mean you almost croaked at the sight of him?" she teased to cover her chaotic emotions.

"Yes. He reminded me of some of those men with the black hair in *The Godfather* films. You know the kind I mean?"

Sydney knew exactly what she meant. He had the look of some Mediterranean types she'd met in her travels.

"Except that his eyes were green like my cat's."

For the second time in one evening Sydney felt light-headed.

When a priest went on vacation, could he remove his collar without it being a sin? Could they vacation alone? Didn't they go to retreats that were off limits to the public? Sydney had no idea.

Beyond his work as a priest, and the fact that his first name was Jarod, she knew nothing personal about Father Kendall. She had no knowledge of his history, where he came from, or whether he had family still living.

"Did he specifically seek you out to ask about me?"

"I'm not sure. He saw my junior ranger name

tag and said he once knew a woman from Cannon who'd become a park ranger.

"When I asked him what her name was, he said Sydney Taylor. I told him I'd been working with you this summer. He wondered if you were around. When I told him you were at a wedding in California, he asked where you lived so he could leave you a note."

So that was how it had happened.

"Did you get it?"

Sydney's hand tightened on the phone. "I'm afraid not." In the next breath she told Cindy about her move to Gardiner and her new job.

The teen sounded terribly disappointed by the news, but Sydney promised to stay in close touch with her and the other kids throughout the year. Slightly mollified, Cindy said she was glad, then she brought their conversation back to Father Kendall.

"Could that man be one of your old boyfriends?"

"No—" Sydney cried before she realized how emotional that would have sounded to Cindy. "I'm thinking he was probably a parent of one of my students, but I just don't remember. It doesn't matter. I'll talk to you again soon if that's all right."

"Oh sure. 'Bye for now."

Sydney hung up, still trembling. Father Kendall had gone to a lot of trouble to come to the park to find her. For what reason?

Feeling trapped and desperate, Sydney got ready for bed, then collapsed on top of the mattress, sobbing.

The next time she had any awareness of her surroundings, she was shivering. At first she was so dazed by the haunting dream where she'd spent the night with Father Kendall at the rectory in Cannon, she assumed she was suffering overwhelming guilt for what she'd done in the dream.

Then to her chagrin she realized she'd slept all night on top of the covers. She couldn't seem to throw off the effects of the dream which had been too real. No doubt her body was still reacting to the feel of him as he'd picked her up and carried her into the apartment last night.

The physical contact coming so unexpectedly in her weakened condition had set off shock waves. They were growing stronger in intensity because she knew Father Kendall was still somewhere around, waiting to take advantage of her vulnerability.

Jarred into action by the fear of seeing him

again and being unable to resist him, she flew to the bathroom for a quick shower. After shampooing her hair, she toweled it dry and put on a clean pair of jeans and a knit blue top.

Once she'd applied lipstick and brushed her hair, she grabbed her purse and opened the apartment door to leave. In the next instant she almost collided with a solid male frame and felt strong hands grip her upper arms to steady her.

For the second time since last night, Sydney lifted her head and discovered Father Kendall, freshly shaved, staring down at her.

Breathless for several reasons, she eased out of his arms. This morning he was dressed in a burgundy-toned polo shirt and faded denims.

There wasn't a man in existence to equal his striking dark looks and physique. In fact nothing compared to the sight of his vital, living presence in a spot where she couldn't have imagined seeing him in a dozen lifetimes.

Her unrealistic hope that she'd be gone from the apartment before he came to her door hadn't materialized of course. Deep in her core she'd known this moment was inevitable. Until she agreed to talk to him, he wouldn't give her any peace.

Instead of attempting to avoid him, she'd be

wise to find out what he wanted and get this over with. Otherwise her turmoil would destroy her.

Having made that decision, she drew in air to help steady her equilibrium while she faced this man who'd dominated her mind and heart far too long for her emotional well-being.

"What is it you want?" she asked in a resigned voice though her heart was frantically beating in her throat.

Jarod remained in place, his narrowed eyes trained on her features in the morning light.

"I'm glad you realize we have to talk, Sydney."

She rubbed her damp palms nervously against her jeans-clad hips. His gaze took in the telling gesture.

"I'm due at school right now and won't be free until four."

"I'll pick you up here at four-fifteen."

He had her cornered.

She was fascinated by the tiny nerve that pulsed at the side of his jaw. Because he'd once worn a beard, she'd never seen the lower half of his facial features bared to her gaze until now. If anything he was more appealing, more...human somehow.

More tempting.

This was all wrong, but he'd left her no choice.

"All right."

Maybe she was mistaken, but she thought she saw a gleam of satisfaction darken his eyes before he accompanied her to her car and watched her drive off. Like a master puppeteer, he had all the power to pull her strings.

The rest of her day passed in a tension-filled blur before she found herself back at her apartment and in his company once more.

She averted her eyes and headed toward an unfamiliar blue car she could see parked out in front of the complex. While they walked, she felt his piercing gaze on her profile.

How strange was fate that he'd actually stepped from her dreams into her reality. During the school year she'd spent in Cannon, they'd never planned a prearranged rendezvous to be alone together. Had never been on a date. This would be the one and only exception.

She kept telling herself maybe this final meeting was what they both needed to settle their unfinished business. Once he left Gardiner for good, they could get on with their separate lives and not look back. This would be the closure she desperately needed.

Out of the periphery she noticed his black hair

was longer than she'd remembered. When he returned to his duties without his beard, the parish would notice the changes in him and be stunned.

She swallowed hard. There couldn't be a more attractive man alive anywhere. His over-whelming physical appeal forced her to hold on to the open car door for a moment while she waited to get control of her emotions.

"You look incredibly beautiful, Sydney."

The first words to come out of his mouth left her tongue-tied so that her response was unintelligible. He'd destroyed the myth that she could ever forget him. In fact his intimate observation acted like a verbal assault on her senses. During those nine months in Cannon he'd rarely spoken his private thoughts…except through his lambent green eyes.

Avoiding his gaze, she climbed inside. Afraid he would touch her and realize the true state of her feelings, she tried her best to elude him, but her arm accidentally brushed against his chest anyway. At the first contact, unaccustomed desire stole through her body.

She still had a hard time believing he'd come to Montana, that she was about to drive off somewhere alone with him.

A couple of the tenants waved and smiled at her. They could see she was in the company of a tall, dark stranger.

She nodded to them before Father Kendall closed the door. He walked around the car and levered himself inside behind the wheel. She could feel his eyes on her.

"Living in an apartment is like living in a goldfish bowl much the same way I once lived back in Cannon."

Once?

Surprised by the revelation, her head swiveled around so she could look at him. He started the car and headed out of town.

"Does that mean you've been transferred to another parish?"

She heard his abrupt intake of breath. "I'd prefer to wait until we arrive at our destination before answering your questions. If you'll reach around on the back seat, I brought us hamburgers and fries. I thought we could eat en route."

En route to where?

Sydney had thought he was taking her out to dinner. His cryptic statements were unsettling enough, but it was his mysterious behavior that was beginning to alarm her.

Thankful for something to eat that might take the edge off her frayed nerves, she undid the seat belt long enough to retrieve the large sack. Inside she found two colas and several portions of cheesecake packed with the food. She put the drinks in the holders between their seats, then handed him his meal.

After thanking her, he began eating with what seemed a healthy appetite, as if this were an everyday occurrence for him. Normally she was hungry after work of any kind, but right now her emotions made her stomach clench. She could only eat a few bites.

"This tastes good," she finally murmured if only to fill the unsettling silence.

"You've hardly touched your food."

Ignoring his observation, she cleaned everything up and put the sack on the floor of the back seat.

Shadows formed by the pines were growing longer. Soon night would fall.

A tangible quiet filled the car during the drive. She could hardly breathe for the tension between them. Though he was a stranger here, he seemed to know his way around.

He drove them into the little town of Ennis.

In a few minutes they came to a tiny, white, nondenominational church partially hidden by giant jack pines. There were no cars or people. He pulled into the parking area around the side where they were away from the street, then he shut off the motor.

Once again he'd surprised Sydney by coming to this particular spot. Maybe she'd been wrong about his reasons for seeking her out. If that was the case, and he'd wanted to talk to her in a holy place, why a church located on the other side of town? What was going on? She simply didn't understand him.

Unable to handle the silence any longer, she cried, "Father Kendall—I…I—"

"Don't call me that," he interrupted. "I have no more parish to minister to. I've left the priesthood."

Sydney's body froze.

"*What did you just say?*"

"Two months ago I laid my case before the Church. I'm no longer Father Kendall, and never will be again."

She couldn't comprehend it. The shock was so great, she wasn't able to think or talk.

"I don't question your incredulity, Sydney. If

I hadn't lived through this experience myself, I wouldn't believe it, either. But it's true."

A rush of adrenaline drove her out of the car where she could breathe in fresh air and try to process what he'd just told her. She stood beside the car hugging her arms to her waist.

When he approached, she lifted tormented eyes to him. "*Why* did you leave?"

A stillness came over him. He studied her features for what seemed like an eternity. "You already know the answer to that question. I fell in love with you."

Like the thrust of a lance, overwhelming guilt pierced her soul. Her body shook. "No—please tell me that wasn't the reason."

Lines darkened his face, making him appear older. "You were there when it happened because you fell in love with me, too. We suffered nine months in silence. Tonight I've broken that silence."

Tears slipped down her cheeks. "It's all my fault—" Her voice rang throughout the pines.

His jaw hardened. "What are you talking about?"

"After the first time I took Brenda to your office, I should never have gone with her again.

When she told me she wouldn't go for any more counseling sessions unless I accompanied her, I clung to that excuse so I could see you. But deep in my heart, I knew it was wrong.

"For that whole school year I deluded myself into believing I hadn't crossed the line with you. But I *did* cross it!" she cried. "I crossed it every time I found a legitimate way to be with you."

"We both crossed it, Sydney. I made certain we could be together under all possible circumstances."

His confession caused her to groan out loud. "If I'd been a stronger person, I would have stolen away from Cannon without your ever knowing about it. Instead I sought you out one last time. I shouldn't have done that."

There'd been a price to pay for the kiss of desperation they'd exchanged. Only now was she beginning to understand the far-reaching ramifications of her actions.

By now moisture dripped off her chin. "L-last night I thought you came to-to—"

"I know what you thought," he cut in. "You had every right to assume what you did."

She buried her face in her hands. "I'm a horrible person. I threw temptation in the face of a man who'd pledged himself to a life of celibacy. I can't bear it that I'm the reason you gave up your vocation.

"You're such a wonderful priest. When I think about all the good you've done, your kindness and understanding in handling Brenda who'd wanted to get an abortion. Because of your guidance and advice, she gave her baby up for adoption. I'm so ashamed of my actions. To think my reckless behavior has led you to this—" She swung her head around.

"You can't do it, Jarod! You have to go back and tell them you made a mistake. I'm sure hundreds of other celibate priests have had to overcome periods of temptation. It's only human and normal. Your superiors will understand and be happy you've come to your senses in ti—"

"You don't understand, Sydney," he cut her off. "I *have* come to my senses. I'll always love the Church, but I'm a man in love who wants to be your husband.

"As I told you last evening, I came as soon as I could. Nothing's changed between us except that our feelings have grown stronger. After last night, I have living proof." His voice grated.

Before she could take a step away from him, he slid his hands to her shoulders. "I brought you here to ask you to marry me."

CHAPTER THREE

"*Marry*—"

"Yes. We can exchange vows in this little church by the pastor who officiates here. I've already talked to him."

"Wait—" She put her hands in front of her the way she would do to shield herself from a gale-force wind.

His eyes burst into twin green flames. "I don't want to wait. We've lost time we can never recover. I want to live the rest of my life with you. I want us to have children."

She shook her head and jerked out of his grasp. "You don't know what you're saying!" Her panic increased. "Please hear me out. The only reason I agreed to meet you after work was so that I could try and make up for my selfishness."

"*Sydney*—"

His compassion for her pain shook her. "Please, Jarod—let me finish—"

A grimace marred his features. "Go on."

"Like I once told you, I don't espouse any particular religion, but I honor anyone who does, especially you—a man who's made sacrifices to commit your whole life to God.

"Before you came to pick me up, I'd made up my mind to ask your forgiveness for my past actions. E-especially the latest one."

One dark brow dipped in query. "Latest one?"

"Yes." With the words tripping off her tongue, she told him about her unsuccessful trip to Cannon, with the shattering result that she'd learned he was ill. "I was so afraid it was serious."

"It is serious," he came back intensely. "I'm a man in love."

"Don't keep saying that. In light of the difficulties you face every day in your desire to be a priest, I'm deeply ashamed of what I did.

"The only reason our professional association turned into something more was because I wasn't noble or courageous enough to stay away from you."

"Don't torture yourself, Sydney. If you'd tried

to avoid me, I would have found ways for us to be together."

"That doesn't matter now. You *have* to go back to Cannon for yourself, *and* for me. This time you can fulfill your duties free of any emotional baggage or entanglement where I'm concerned."

"It's too late," he whispered.

"Of course it isn't!" she protested in absolute fear. "You're not thinking rationally right now. Jarod—I don't want to be your stumbling block in life. I couldn't live with myself.

"The greater love was to let you go, which I did when I left Cannon. I've lived without you for fifteen months. Though I gave in to my emotions on Saturday, I honestly can stay away from you a lifetime. I promise I can. One day you'll thank me. Please take me home now."

Without further talk she dashed back to the car and got inside. At this point her whole body was trembling in agony for the part she'd played in Jarod's earthshaking decision. Because of her, he'd left the priesthood he loved. The pain of knowing it was her fault was too much—

In a few minutes he joined her. "Sydney? Look at me."

She kept her head bowed. "I don't want to. You'll always be Father Kendall to me."

"Nevertheless I'm no longer a priest. We finally have the freedom to talk. You can ask me anything you want."

"I don't dare."

"That's because you're afraid."

"It's more than that—a priest doesn't just leave because he's been tempted by a woman."

"Some do if they realize they can't stay focused. When there's no more joy in service, then it's time to go."

She shivered as if someone had just walked over her grave.

"As soon as I met you, I became like Jacob who wrestled with a dark angel. The agony had to stop."

A cry of despair escaped her throat. "But you're too fine a priest to leave. I saw how much the people love, even worship you. I've never known anyone to command such respect and admiration.

"I—I feel ill that our association has caused you to turn your back on the people you've loved." Her head reared so she could look at him. "I *know* you love them!"

"Of course I do. I always will. A part of me will

never forget that I was once Father Kendall. But there's been another part of my body and soul which had lain dormant until you walked into my office. Your arrival into my world became a life changing experience for me. If you're honest, you'll admit you felt the same way."

Heaven help her but she did—

A fire had been lit that first day when she'd accompanied Brenda to his office for counseling. Sydney had been the one to encourage her to seek out her own clergyman. Knowing the girl needed support, Sydney had volunteered to go with her to Brenda's family priest.

When they'd walked in his office, Jarod had looked up. One glance at the striking priest she'd talked to on the phone prior to the appointment and she'd actually felt delicious pain.

That moment would always stay with her. She wiped the moisture off her cheeks. "How did you know I wasn't married yet?"

He eyed her steadily. "It was something I felt in my gut, but I didn't get it confirmed until two months ago when the secretary at Cannonball High School helped me track you down."

She drew in a ragged breath. "How did she manage that?"

"I told her I needed her help to locate Brenda, and wondered if her former English teacher, Ms. Taylor, might still be in touch with her. You probably didn't know Brenda's family moved from Cannon after you left.

"To make a long story short, the secretary phoned the school district office and was given your parents' phone number from your personal history card. She then phoned your mother who told her you'd become a park ranger and worked at Yellowstone.

"The secretary asked if you went by your married name, at which point your mother indicated you were still single."

"I see."

Jarod's resourcefulness shouldn't have surprised her. Even knowing it was wrong, a part of her thrilled to the knowledge that he'd gone to those lengths to learn her whereabouts. What was wrong with her?

"It's been a long time since we last saw each other, Sydney. Long enough for another man to be in your life."

The definite edge to his possessive tone sent another shiver racing up her spine.

"I considered marrying a man who works for

the forest service." She bowed her head. "But in the end I—"

"You couldn't commit because of me," he cut off the rest of her words with what sounded like a groan of satisfaction.

Since what he'd said was patently true, Sydney couldn't deny it, yet she couldn't believe any of this was happening.

"Jarod—we can't do this—"

"Do what?" he came back with unfathomable calm.

"Be together."

"Give me one reason why not."

A half sob lodged in her throat. "Because it's wrong! I can't view you the same way I would any other man."

"I should hope not."

His wry response tied her up in knots.

"You know what I mean," she cried emotionally. "You've left a whole way of life to be with…me."

"Didn't you mean what you said in my office that last day?"

She squirmed in the seat. "I don't know what you're getting at." What a liar she was!

He sucked in his breath. "You wanted to stay,

but I couldn't ask that of you while I was still ordained. Now that I'm free, there's nothing to hold us back from having a life together.

"We already know how we feel at the deepest level. What we need to do now is be married. We'll have the rest of ours lives to get to know everything else about each other. Nothing but becoming man and wife will satisfy either of us at this point.

"We can go away, live anywhere. If you want to stay here and teach, that's fine. I've already been promised a counseling job in Gardiner to support us if that appeals to you."

"Wait—" she cried. "You're going too fast for me. I need time to think this all out."

He leaned across the seat and caught her chin in his hand. She moaned at his touch. "I love you, Sydney. I did from the very first moments of our meeting. Let's not waste any more time living apart. Life's too short. I long to share it all with you. Just tell me you want a life with me, too."

His warm breath on her lips sent fingers of forbidden yearning through her system.

"If the answer is no, then I'll leave and you'll never see me again."

A cry of pain left her lips. "Does that mean you'll go back to the Church?"

"No." His voice sounded raw. "That part of my life is over."

A new fear seized her heart. "Then what will you do?"

The caress of his fingers against her skin created fire everywhere he touched her. "If you can't bring yourself to marry me, then it shouldn't matter to you where I go or what happens to me."

The mere thought of his leaving where she could never find him was incomprehensible to her.

"*Jarod—*"

"Say the words I need to hear, Sydney." His urgency thrilled yet alarmed her.

"You know I'm so deeply in love with you, my life's been a desolate waste."

"That makes two of us," he whispered against her lips before his mouth started to cover hers, but she turned her head and pushed him away.

"Why won't you let me kiss you?" he whispered against her neck where the scent of her perfume still lingered.

"Because I feel a guilt that runs so deep, I

can't handle it. The man I loved was a priest. I'm still having an impossible time absorbing the revelation that you've left the priesthood. To be honest, I'm terrified."

"Of me?" His voice grated.

"Of course of you. Of me. Of both our feelings. Of all the ramifications!"

She felt the shudder that racked his hard, fit body before he removed his hands from her arms and sat back in the seat.

"How can I take your fear away, Sydney? I was a man long before I became a priest."

"You weren't a normal man, Jarod. You felt a calling which separated you from other men. It drove you to make vows to God you intended to keep for a lifetime…until I came along," she half sobbed. "Our situation reminds me of a book I read in my teens about a woman who fell in love with a man while she was vacationing in the Sahara.

"They went on a journey together. But her ecstasy changed to agony when she learned he was a monk who'd run away from the monastery.

"Their happiness together vanished because he couldn't live with himself after what he'd done. He loved his life as a monk too much.

Until he'd seen her walking in the monastery garden, it had been all he'd known.

"She couldn't live with him under those circumstances. At last she encouraged him to go back to the life he'd always loved. That was the end of the book.

"I sobbed for hours after reading it. To this day I've been haunted about her life, how she managed to live without him after experiencing such intense joy with him."

"I read that book, too," he whispered. "It was a piece of fiction. I'm no monk, and I left the priesthood after asking for permission."

"And did you get it?"

"From the bishop, yes. From the Pope, not yet. Maybe never." Sydney felt her heart fail a little more. "But all you need to understand is that I didn't become a priest for the same reasons the man in the story did."

She shook her head. "It doesn't matter, Jarod. I—I can't deal with this. Please take me home."

To her immense relief, he started the car. They drove in disturbing silence all the way back to Gardiner.

The second he pulled up in front of the apartment, Sydney opened the door and darted toward her unit. Yet Jarod somehow reached it before she did.

"If you'll invite me in, there's a lot I need to tell you, explain to you. I didn't grow up knowing I had a calling to the priesthood. It didn't happen that way for me. I happen to believe life is a great journey. I've traveled down many of its paths, but I've yet to experience the ultimate.

"Though I've loved my life as a priest, I've discovered one key element is still missing. With you, I know I could find it. Think on that before you doom us to a level of existence where it will take everything we have simply to survive."

Tears continued to stream down Sydney's face. "I don't care what you say. All the explanations in the world won't change the fact that I'm the reason you left. I'll never make it through life with that on my conscience.

"I was wrong to have tempted you the way I did—wrong ever to have suggested you come to me—I'll be paying for that sin for the rest of my life. But if you go back now, maybe one day I'll be forgiven."

He eyed her intently. "For a woman who's never gone to church, you wear your guilt like a garment. Why is that, Sydney? Where does all this self-inflicted pain come from? I've made my peace with myself and God. Why isn't that enough for you?"

"I don't want to talk about it anymore."

Jarod chewed on his lower lip. "I'll be waiting for you after school tomorrow. If by that time you still can't bring yourself to listen to me, then I'm leaving on Thursday morning, and I won't be back. But if you let me walk away, you'll discover that your life isn't complete, either, and never will be."

She watched his long powerful legs eat up the expanse. After he drove off, she still stood there trembling. Partly from the cold night air, but mostly from his prophecy, which touched a chord deep inside her.

He was right.

Her life hadn't been complete since meeting him. It would never be complete without him.

But in order to live with him, she would have to marry an *ex-priest*.

Visions of him in his collar and vestments saying Mass and giving communion flashed through her mind.

How was she supposed to separate those images from the man who'd just left her wearing a polo shirt and jeans? They were two different men in the same body.

He said he loved her more than the priesthood. But after they married, how long would it take before he realized his mistake and yearned for his former life?

Terrified over the prospect, she dashed inside her apartment more tormented than ever. Her heart was weighted with too many questions for which there were no answers, except one.

She did love him beyond all else.

Yet in this case was her love enough to hold and keep him?

That burning question was the one torturing her now. If Sydney ever had to give him up like the woman in the story, she wouldn't want to go on living... She'd done it once and she knew she didn't have the strength to do it again.

Before Jarod reached the motel, his cell phone rang.

Sydney?

But one glance at the caller ID extinguished that hope. He clicked on. "Rick?"

"Is this bad timing?"

"Not at all," Jarod muttered.

"Have you been with Sydney?"

He closed his eyes tightly. "I have."

The image of those first moments was indelibly engraved in his memory. One glimpse of the hunger in her eyes and he didn't worry about the frozen expression of her features. She'd gone so still he was able to trace the perfect symmetry of her oval face.

Every time she'd come to his office in the past, he'd studied those same unforgettable features and straight nose that gave her so much character.

Tonight his gaze had followed the lines of those lovely bones beneath a complexion that had turned pale despite her suntan. Her sculpted mouth looked drained of its natural pink tinge.

All her color had seemed to be pooled in those dark-fringed eyes whose myriad of rainbow flecks reflected the blue tone of the cotton sweater she was wearing. They pulsated with life though the rest of her body had gone perfectly still.

She'd emanated a quiet anger that would have daunted him if he didn't know through years of counseling that anger masked many emotions. He'd wanted to surprise her in order to judge her first reaction. Whatever she felt, she hadn't been indifferent to him. He'd needed that much positive reinforcement to counterbalance his own deep-seated fears.

"Did her reaction tell you everything you needed to know?"

"That and a great deal more than I had imagined…"

"You sound like you're in torment."

"I've given her until Thursday to find the courage to really face me."

"What happens if she can't?"

"I haven't asked myself that question yet. How is Father Lane handling everything?" He needed to change the subject or go a little mad in the process.

"I say this in charity. He's trying his best, but Father Kendall's shoes are impossible to fill. The phone has been ringing off the hook. Kay says everyone in the parish wants to know where you are and when you'll be back. Before this place explodes, the hierarchy needs to make some kind of announcement soon."

Jarod bowed his head. "All anyone needs to

know is that I'm on retreat. Give it another couple of months and things will settle down."

"That's what you say, but I don't think so."

"How's Kay?"

"If you mean, how did she react when I told her the news, she cried all night. By morning she'd recovered enough to tell me she loves you more for knowing your own heart and doing something about it. She knew I was going to phone you, and told me she was praying you and Sydney will get together."

"Coming from your wife that means a lot, Rick."

"I'm sending my prayers with hers."

"I'll need them," Jarod admitted. "Sydney blames herself for my leaving. She has begged me to go back before it's too late."

"That's only natural. You've had fifteen months to consider your actions. She needs time for the shock to wear off."

He rubbed his forehead. "I've counseled hundreds of people, but I've never met anyone whose guilt runs as deep as hers. To be honest, I'm not at all certain she'll be able to let it go."

"A conscience like that is revealing of her true nature. No wonder you love her."

"She's exceptional."

"So are you. Somehow I have to believe you'll get together."

"After seeing her again, I can't fathom going through life without her."

"The power of love can work miracles."

"I'm going to hang on to those words, Rick. Thanks for calling."

"Don't forget I'm always here if you need to talk."

"That goes both ways. Good night."

Jarod hung up the phone, immobilized by the real possibility that the power of love wasn't going to be enough.

Aware Jarod would be waiting for her when back-to-school night was over, Sydney's nerves were so fragile, she jumped when the bell for seventh period rang.

The last group of parents and students filed in her classroom. She greeted each one and handed them a disclosure. She was about to shut the door to give her presentation when one more person approached.

"*Jarod*—" Sydney cried in startled surprise when she saw who it was.

"At least you didn't call me Father Kendall. That's progress," he said in a low aside. His bold gaze made a swift appraisal of her face and figure clothed in a navy skirt and blazer.

Heat swept into her face.

All day she'd been anxious and keyed up knowing they'd be together before the night was over. But it completely threw her that he would come into the school.

Dressed in another suit, this time of charcoal-gray with a white shirt and pearl-gray tie, he was so good-looking, he eclipsed all the men in the room. Everyone stared at him, particularly the mothers and female students who were mesmerized by the gorgeous male stranger in their midst.

They'd all be shocked to learn that until very recently, he'd worn a collar and black robes.

"May I?" he murmured, taking the last paper from her hands. Before she knew it, he'd found a place to sit at the back of the room next to Steve Carr and his parents. Steve had been one of her junior rangers.

"Hey there, Syd—" The cute high school senior gave her a big grin.

She nodded to him, wishing he hadn't acknowledged her like that in front of Jarod who noticed everything and might start up a conversation with him.

Sydney didn't want anyone to know about the priest from her past, especially not Steve whose dad was a ranger. Talk spread like wildfire among the other rangers. The less anyone knew about her personal life, the better. Then she wouldn't have to face the questions when it was all over.

By some miracle she made her way to the front of the class without stumbling. After giving her little speech about the year's curriculum, followed by her expectations of participation and behavior, the principal's voice came over the loudspeaker.

"We want to thank all the parents for coming. We'll look forward to seeing your children bright and early Monday morning to begin another exciting school year. Until then, enjoy your long Labor Day weekend."

Most of the students in the room made a face before clustering around Sydney's desk. Since they knew her from their many visits to the Park throughout the year, they were excited to discover she'd left her job as a ranger to teach them English.

Though she was flattered by their interest,

and tried to pay attention, her gaze kept straying to Jarod who was in conversation with Steve and his parents. At this point they would know he wasn't a parent. That in itself would raise speculation about his presence.

Seeing him in the back of the room made her realize that he really wasn't a priest anymore. Until this moment, nothing about his arrival in Gardiner had seemed real.

Her heart pounded unmercifully to realize that since he'd made the decision to leave the priesthood, he was free to go where he wanted, do what he wanted. He'd given her until tomorrow morning to make a decision about marrying him. If the answer was no, she would never see him again.

But how could she say *yes* when she had so many fears? Yet how could she possibly let him go when she was so painfully in love with him?

Little by little the room emptied until they were alone. He strolled toward her, bigger than life.

"Your students are crazy about you, especially Steve Carr. You're a natural with people, young or old."

"Thank you," she whispered while she straightened her desk.

"What did you tell him about yourself?"

"That I'm a counselor and am considering settling down here in Gardiner. I refrained from informing him I plan to marry his teacher as soon as possible."

Her breath caught.

"Is there anything I can help you do before we leave?"

"No—I'm ready."

"Good. Then I'll follow you home and we'll go to dinner."

"No—" she cried jerkily. "I'd rather we weren't seen together socially." The fact that he'd shown up at her classroom tonight was bad enough. Going out to dinner would generate more gossip. After he left Gardiner, she didn't relish making explanations to any more people than she had to.

His eyes gleamed. "Fine. I much prefer talking to you at your apartment." He reached the door and flipped off the switch. "After you, Sydney."

She could hardly breathe as she moved past him and they made their way down the side stairs to the nearest exit. They passed a few teachers and parents. Sydney smiled at them, but kept walking at a brisk pace so no one would detain her. The less explanations to anyone about the attractive male at her side, the better.

After escorting her to her car, he followed in his blue rental. Her apartment was only a few streets away. By the time he pulled in one of the visitor stalls and came around to help her, her heart was pounding out of control. She could hardly move her limbs. Being this near to him made her go weak with desire, but always accompanying it was this stabbing guilt.

He looked down at her from veiled eyes. "Shall I get in the passenger side so we can talk, or are you going to invite me inside your place?"

"I-it would be better if you just left now," she stammered.

Though they weren't touching, she felt his body stiffen. "You never want to see me again. Is that what you're saying?"

She shook her head in despair. "I want you to go back to Cannon."

Jarod's eyes grew bleak. "But it's not what I want."

Heartsick she cried, "You wanted it once, or you would never have taken your vows. It's too late."

"Shall we continue talking here where

everyone in the complex can hear us?" he reminded her in a low voice.

He was right. Since she'd driven in, two other tenants had come out to their cars.

Summoning her strength, she got out of the driver's seat and hurried past him toward her apartment. While she unlocked the door, he followed at a slower pace.

In a final effort to be strong, she barred the entry, letting him know she didn't want him to come in.

"I've had time to think it over. I won't be the person who's responsible for ruining your life. One day you'll thank me. Time and a change of scene without me is what you need to come to your senses."

"Sydney—" His voice sounded like it was reaching out to her from deep inside a dark cavern.

She trembled despite her resolve. "This has to be goodbye, Jarod."

In a move of desperation, she closed the door and locked it.

Sydney listened for his car. When she finally heard the sound of the motor and knew he'd driven off, she staggered over to the couch where she collapsed in despair.

Her loss was so great, she couldn't bear it. Great heaving sobs broke from her body.

The dream she'd dreamed of his giving up the priesthood for her had come true. This was the real thing. But it had turned into a nightmare.

How could she marry him knowing the part she'd played in his decision?

Beset by new fears, she cried uncontrollably. What tormented her now was the knowledge that he intended to live in the world like any other normal man. It meant he'd meet other people, other *women*, any of whom would give everything they had to be his wife if they were lucky enough to be loved by him.

I want to live the rest of my life with you, Sydney. I want us to have children.

So what if he got her pregnant, then later on wrestled with his desire to be a priest again?

That part of my life is over.

He could say that now, but when he'd taken his vows, he'd meant to honor them forever, too.

How did she know that in a year or five years, he wouldn't change his mind again and want to go back? Then she and their child would become the obstacle in his path to true happiness.

That would mean she was twice responsible

for his pain. She would lose him twice. While she was still reeling with her own debilitating pain, she thought she heard a knock at the door.

She lifted her head from where she'd been lying in a crumpled heap to listen.

"Sydney?" came Jarod's urgent voice.

She thought he'd gone a long time ago.

"I've been listening to you crying. Let me in, or I swear I'll break this door down."

CHAPTER FOUR

"PLEASE DON'T DO that!" One thing Sydney knew about Jarod. He would carry out his threat.

She leaped from the couch and hurried over to the door to open it, but her eyelids were so swollen, she could hardly see out of her eyes.

This time Jarod didn't wait for her permission to come inside. After closing the door behind him, he turned to her with a forbidding expression.

"I promise not to come near you or touch you, but you're not getting rid of me until you've at least heard me out."

Jarod exerted such a powerful force, she was helpless to defy him any further.

"W-would you like some coffee first?"

"I'd love some, but I'll make it."

She could just imagine how ghastly she looked after her long crying jag. It was humiliating to realize he'd been outside the whole time, privy to her anguish.

"All right," she murmured. "I'll freshen up and be back in a minute."

Once in her bedroom, she changed into jeans and a dark green cotton sweater, then she went in the bathroom to wash her face and brush her hair. After applying lipstick, she felt a little more prepared to face him.

When she went back to the living room, she found him standing there drinking from a mug. Hers was on the coffee table. She picked it up before sitting down in the overstuffed chair next to the couch. While he eyed her movements, she tried her hardest to avoid his direct gaze.

"I was a man first, Sydney."

She swallowed some of the hot liquid before answering him. "I've heard that a lot of priests have an affinity for the priesthood early in life," she whispered.

"Nothing so romantic happened to me. The truth is, I come from a dysfunctional Long Island, New York, family and I don't recall the last time any of them stepped inside a church.

"Until late into graduate school, I could never

have imagined joining any church, let alone giving up women."

The unexpected information shattered all Sydney's preconceived notions concerning his path to the priesthood.

"Ever heard of Kendall Mills?"

Sydney blinked. Every household in America baked with Kendall Mills flour. He was *that* Kendall? They had to be worth millions, maybe even billions.

"I—I don't think I want to know anything more," she said in a throbbing voice.

"That's because you've had me on some kind of pedestal and don't want to find out I'm not the saint you've envisioned. But we can't hope to have a life together if you never let me explain my past."

There could be no future. She knew she couldn't make him give up everything for her, but she was starving for information about him because she loved him so terribly.

Defeated for the moment, she bowed her head.

"I realize you're terrified of the man behind the robes," he said with a compassion she didn't want to feel. "You know all about the priest, but you know nothing about Jarod Kendall, the man."

"It doesn't matter, Jarod. The Church would take you back again—" She couldn't prevent more tears from falling. "Whatever you've done, you can explain to them, tell them you've made a mistake—"

She heard a sound come out of him that could have been anguish or frustration, probably both.

"I didn't make a mistake when I decided to become a priest. I haven't made one by leaving, After you've heard what I have to say, you'll view things differently. Tonight I intend to tell you everything I couldn't speak of while I was still ordained."

Because she could feel her defenses crumbling, it scared her to listen to any more explanations. When she'd known him as a priest, he'd been shrouded in mystery. It had added to her fascination of the mystique surrounding him.

To hear it all bared…

Sydney cupped her mug and drank thirstily as if the steaming brew would somehow fortify her against the power of his forthcoming revelations.

"Several of my mentors in the seminary felt the call as early as adolescence. Not so with me. In fact I can't pinpoint the exact moment when I knew I wanted to be a priest."

Their gazes met. "Do you remember in my office when you told me that organized religion meant nothing to you, Sydney? I could have told you I felt the same way growing up."

She averted her head. After all their history together, it was so hard to hear this kind of truth come out of him.

"When I think about it, I suppose my journey began as a gradual process that started in my mid-teens. I had a big group of good friends, but it was my best friend Matt Graham with whom I spent the most time. Matt happened to be a Catholic who played on the parish basketball team in East Hampton where we all lived.

"Occasionally I went to practice with him and did his homework for him while I waited. One of the younger, energetic priests, Father Pyke, noticed me sitting on the sidelines and insisted I join them. He said my height and natural athleticism would be the added weapon they needed against the other teams in the diocese.

"Since I found it harder and harder to go

home after school and hear mother crying in the bedroom, I hung around the church gym with Matt quite a bit."

Sydney cringed, sensing some awful revelation was about to be disclosed.

"Before long I found myself confiding in the priest about the problems plaguing my family. Obviously I needed an outlet to ease my pain, especially because my brother and sister were both away at college.

"Since I didn't want to confide in my friends, Father Pyke was the lucky one who got to hear my sorrows. I found a certain comfort in realizing I could talk to him and know it wouldn't go any further. Looking back at that particularly difficult time with my family, I can see why I was drawn to him.

"He was a great listener. When he heard the ugly truth about my father being a womanizer, he didn't patronize me with empty platitudes."

A groan came out of Sydney. Hearing this was too painful.

"My parents are socially prominent people who've always had a hectic agenda that has kept them running from one event to another with no regard for their children's emotional needs.

"Little by little I told the priest all our ugly secrets. I was hurt and angry over my father's behavior because it wounded my mother who drank too much. The fighting between them was getting worse.

"At one point my mother told me the latest woman my father had been seeing was married, making an awful situation even more reprehensible. Yet she wouldn't think of leaving him because they both needed each other's family money more than they craved peace or honor."

Jarod was painting a horror story that would have been too much for any child to bear. Moisture dripped off Sydney's cheeks.

"I'm so sorry, Jarod."

"You can't comprehend it, can you. Sydney? At the time, neither could I," he said with a profound sadness that went bone deep. "For one thing, our family has been in the Hamptons for generations. Because of that fact, a lot of people know my parents, or know of them. Intermingled with my pain was the shame I felt that they were the major topic of conversation behind closed doors."

She cringed. No boy or girl should have to

live with that kind of hurt. The tragic picture he was painting devastated Sydney who couldn't help but contrast his upbringing with her own happy home. Though there'd been differences of opinion on certain issues from time to time, there'd been no strife between her parents to destroy her security.

"Worse, Matt's father worked on Wall Street. Both our families moved in the same social circles. To avoid humiliating questions, I stopped going over to his house. In time the church gym or the priest's study became the only places I felt safe from gossip for the rest of my high school experience.

"After graduation Matt and I, plus a few other friends, traveled around Europe for the summer. We met women, we played and partied to our heart's content. After three months of freedom from family problems, I was thankful to be starting Yale on a full academic scholarship for my undergraduate studies."

Sydney knew him to be an extremely intelligent man. His admission only increased her admiration for him in the midst of so much heartache.

"My father had always hoped I would attend Princeton like my elder brother Drew, and join the family business after graduation. Liz was at Wellesley. But I wanted to go to a place where the Kendall name didn't precede me at every turn. My father hated it that I didn't need to rely on his money for my education."

She shook her head. It was ghastly. All of it.

"He expected me to attend law school and take my place in the family corporation. But I was so chagrined over the strained relations with my parents and siblings who didn't want to talk about our family's problems, I found myself drawn to classes in psychology.

"My struggle to understand the dynamics driving my unhappy parents dominated any other plans I might have had."

"I can understand that," she murmured.

"At one point in my studies, a guest lecturer who happened to be a priest from St. Paul, Minnesota, well known for his successful counseling techniques, taught for a semester. His insights into people and relationships within the family unit captured my interest.

"During my last talk with him at the end of the semester, he suggested I attend seminary in St. Paul which combined earning a masters degree in professional counseling. I laughed and offered the comment that if I were Catholic, the idea would make a lot of sense to me."

With every revelation, Sydney's astonishment grew.

"I never saw him again and went on to graduate, at which point I broke up with the woman I'd been living with for a year."

Living with? For a whole year?

"W-why didn't you stay together?" Sydney couldn't help asking, already insanely jealous of the other woman's place in his life for that amount of time.

He flicked her a penetrating glance. "For the same reason you didn't end up marrying Chip. I wasn't in love with her, and she wanted to get married."

His counter effectively silenced her.

"As soon as graduation was over, I returned to East Hampton and asked Father Pyke to teach me what I had to do to join the Church. In less than a year, I was baptized, confirmed, and received the Eucharist at the same time.

"To my father's angry disbelief, not to mention the rest of my family's utter humiliation and bewilderment over my decision, I left for St. Martha's ministerial college in St. Paul where it all came together for me, setting me on a path that seemed to have chosen me."

So that was how it had happened.

By now Sydney was on her feet, unable to sit still. The unvarnished truth was so different from her erroneous conjectures, she didn't know what to say or think.

"The visiting priest who'd shown such an interest in me at Yale took me under his wing. Once I was ready to assume my duties, we talked about possible places I might go to.

"He told me there was a parish in Cannon, North Dakota, which had been in need of a priest for some time. He painted a charming picture of the Cannonball River of Lewis and Clark fame that flowed across the scenic plains past that rural southwestern community which had grown from a fort.

"I must admit that after the background and bitterness I'd come from, the idea of serving a population of 900 people of multidenominations who made up the little town, delighted me.

"Its reputation for Midwestern ethics of strong moral values and hard work held an irresistible appeal for someone who'd seen the opposite in action within the walls of my own home.

"After the bishop of the Bismarck diocese interviewed me, I was excited to be assigned there. That was ten years ago.

"In the beginning I determined to know my congregation's hopes and fears, joys and sorrows. I lived in the midst of them, performed wedding ceremonies, baptized babies, counseled families and individuals.

"During the first eight years of my ministry, those things hadn't been a distraction from prayer, but a source of my prayers. For me the parish was a sacrament, the window through which I found and viewed myself.

"To my satisfaction the numbers swelled after my arrival. I'd never been happier or enjoyed life more. Every minute was a joy…until I met one Sydney Taylor…"

A stab of fresh pain drove Sydney to bury her face in her hands.

"No man enjoys looking at a beautiful woman more than I do. I've known and dated many women both at home and abroad. Some of those relationships were intimate."

He'd lived with someone for a whole year… Did she know the real Jarod at all?

"But marriage never entered my mind. It

seems my parents' battle-scarred marriage did more damage to me than I realized, putting me off the institution that had locked the two people I loved in mortal combat.

"Later on when the time came for me to take the vow of celibacy, it hardly made a ripple on the surface of my consciousness. The carnal side of my nature had already been indulged to my satisfaction. I'd been fed.

"For me, the most important vow I took was the private one I made to myself, knowing it would be my greatest challenge. I vowed to help make a difference in the lives of other people since I hadn't been able to fix my own parents' problems."

He paused to study her for a breathless moment. "Yet eight years later, I found out that wasn't my greatest challenge. Upon a first meeting with you, it took all of one second to feel the force of physical attraction again.

"When you and Brenda walked in my office, I took one look at you and my heart literally stopped for a moment. By the time you left, I felt an ache that has never gone away. I battled with my feelings after I let you go and I realized the thing had happened my mentors had warned me about when I thought I knew it all."

"Don't say any more!" she cried.

"I have to finish this, Sydney."

She wanted to run away, but there was no place to hide.

"I remember the precise moment in seminary that I mocked Father McQueen inwardly when his subject for the day was 'the temptation of the flesh.'"

Sydney shuddered.

"The older priest's choice of words sounded as if he'd lifted them straight out of Victor Hugo's *Hunchback of Notre Dame*. But I stopped mocking Father McQueen's words from the moment I met *you*, Sydney.

"With the chemistry so overpowering between us, I realized your feelings for me were equally profound."

They were.

"Over the weeks and months you were in Cannon, I tried to fight my desire for you, but no battle was ever won. Ours was a love that had caught on fire. Incredibly, that ache never went away.

"If remaining in pain was my punishment,

then it became too much to bear. My ministry began to suffer even though the parishioners might not have been aware of my turmoil.

"But I didn't fool everyone. My friend Rick Olsen knew something was wrong. Sometimes I caught him looking at me with a solemn, even pained expression. I had reached the zenith of my agony and couldn't remain in that state any longer."

Sydney nodded. She'd thought she could forget by leaving Cannon the moment her teaching contract was up. But it had been a horrendous fifteen months since she'd left.

"Your little trip to Cannon the other day proves we're still burning for each other," he said the words she'd been afraid to say. "Every moment after you left, I struggled to get back my *joie de vivre*. But it didn't happen. Each day became increasingly more impossible to get through.

"The need to see you was so acute, I felt ill. It was a sickness of body and spirit. For the first time in my life I'd fallen in love with a woman. Yet because of my vows, I couldn't do anything about it. I struggled with that pain, Sydney, but now I have left the past behind me, for a future with you."

Sydney understood that feeling better than anyone else.

"After Christmas the thoughts I'd been entertaining to leave the priesthood wouldn't let me alone. Certain things happened I could no longer ignore."

"What things?" She was so caught up in his confession, she couldn't stop herself.

He bowed his head. "Before the Holidays, the Church sent funds for me to purchase a repossessed house from the bank at a good price. It would serve as the new rectory. I wanted the extra space to be put to good use, so I invited my newly married deacon to move in and occupy the top floor.

"One morning about two months ago I let myself in the house through a side entrance. It was so quiet inside, I assumed I was the only one there.

"I walked back to my suite of rooms on the main floor for some brochures I'd left in my study by accident. When I found them, I made my way down the hall to the kitchen for a cup of coffee. I'd decided I could use one before I returned to the office for the rest of the afternoon.

"The door was ajar, so I had no advance warning of what I would see through the aperture. The sight of Rick and his wife Kay in a passionate clinch by the fridge trapped the air in my lungs.

"I turned away, but not before I saw Rick's hands roam over her body and heard her moan of pleasure."

Sydney bit her lip so hard, it drew blood.

"That image drove me out into the ninety-degree heat. Combined with the humidity, it had felt more like a hundred when I'd first driven home. But the awful emptiness attacking me right then made me oblivious to the elements.

"It came to me what a mistake it had been to allow the Olsens to share space in the rectory with me. Since I was the only ordained priest serving the parish, I'd thought the practical thing to help solve their newlywed financial worries was to let them live there for a time and pay a modest rent.

"But as I'd already found out, two people in love can't stay away from each other no matter how hard they try. Such a thing isn't possible. Seeing Kay in Rick's arms drove that point home as never before.

"It wasn't the first time I'd managed to come upon them when they didn't know I was there.

I knew it wouldn't be the last. They'd been like honeymooners since moving in, though they'd always been very careful not to be demonstrative in front of me.

"As I drove away from the house, I realized I had to do something about an untenable situation. After you left Cannon, I awakened every day to a void that was yawning deeper and blacker."

So did I.

They stared at each other. "What a bitter irony that part of my ministry involves counseling people on a constant basis, yet it's the counselor who's in crisis now.

"I thought if I could find information about you—if I knew you belonged to someone else—maybe the knowledge would help extinguish the flame that's been burning hotter and brighter despite everything I've done to put forbidden thoughts away."

He drew in a harsh breath. "You have the kind of beauty that makes a man stop in his tracks. I couldn't imagine you not being married after this long a time. I figured you might even have a child."

Now Sydney's breathing had grown ragged.

"I never believed I could cross the line to get involved with a married woman. I could never have imagined sinking as low as my own father. Yet after labeling him with silent accusations, I realized I wasn't that different from him in my thoughts. I despised myself for my weakness where you're concerned, Sydney.

"In my resolve to have answers one way or the other, I drove to the high school. Out of desperation I used one of my parishioners, Jeanine, who works in the office, to get me the information I needed.

"I told her a deliberate lie. But I had an excuse, I beg you to forgive me because I had to find you." His voice throbbed.

"While Jeanine did some detective work, she thought that you might be teaching in a nearby town, but I doubted it.

"After the way we'd parted, I had the gut feeling you'd moved out of state and were now married to a man who enjoyed all the privileges of being your husband…including the right to share with you what Rick and Kay had been doing earlier."

Jarod's words sent a thrill of desire through Sydney's body.

"During the torturous wait, I determined that if you were married, I would go on retreat to

Europe for a couple of months' renewal and hope for some kind of epiphany that would help me survive the rest of my life without your memory sapping my joy in the work.

"But if by some miracle you hadn't met a man you wanted to marry yet, then I was at the point where I had to face what it was I really wanted. Even if it meant hurting other people, I knew what I had to do.

"I wanted to be with you," he said in a deep, husky tone.

She weaved in place.

"The second I learned you were still single and working at Yellowstone, my decision was made. After months of trying to fight my natural desires, it became clear I would never win the struggle.

"I owed my superior all the truth in me when I announced I was leaving the priesthood. The very fact that I could say those words aloud should have made me tremble with fear. Instead, I felt like a real man again at the mere idea of seeing my heart's desire, again.

"From that moment on, I never looked back."

Jarod— Could what he was saying really be true?

"It was the measure of how far removed my thoughts were from everything else important to me. Once I'd laid my case before the bishop, I began to make plans.

"I scanned the Yellowstone Park Web site for work possibilities and noticed a link to their Employee Assistance Program. They run a counseling service for their own people. I read the list of skills for the manager position. My qualifications were perfectly suited for the job. Which means I can support you if we decide we want to remain here.

"The head woman, Maureen Scofield, told me it was mine if I wanted it, but I have to let her know soon."

Sydney knew Maureen well. Jarod would have bowled her over.

He raked his hands through his hair. "So now that you know everything, I'm going to ask you one more time to be my wife."

Sydney's heart raced so fast, she could hardly breathe.

"How can I give you an answer when you have no idea how you're going to feel a month or a year from now? Once the first thrill of being together wears off, you'll probably start to compare your level of happiness against the joy you felt serving the parish. No matter what you say, a wife will come in second best.

"Knowing how honorable you are, you'll remain silent even though you'll be dying to ask me for a divorce. I can't fathom how terrible it would be to watch you suffer over a decision you should never have made."

His sensuous mouth flattened to a thin line. "I'll be taking the same risk."

Her head reared. "What do you mean?"

"After a few months, it's possible you'll become disenchanted of married life with me. We've been forbidden fruit to each other, but maybe you'll decide I wasn't everything you desired in a husband."

Her cheeks flamed.

"I'm not going to tire of you, or long for my old life." Shadows darkened his handsome features. "Don't you understand I want to grow old with you?"

"You say that now—" she cried, doubt flooding through her.

His lids lowered so she couldn't read the expression in his eyes. "Forgive me for keeping you up so late." He turned to leave.

"Wait—where are you going?"

He paused midstride. "To the motel."

"You *know* what I meant." She moistened her lips nervously. "What will you do?"

"Without you in my life, I plan to move to Europe to work and live."

The blood pounded in her ears. "Europe?"

"Yes. You and I are going to need an ocean between us. Since I spent some of my happier times there with friends, it makes the most sense. I want a life, Sydney. I crave all the things other men take for granted. A wife…children…

"I wanted you to be the woman I married, but since that isn't possible, then I'll meet someone who can handle the fact that I was once a priest. Someone who wants the same things out of life I do."

His words caused excruciating pain. She took a step closer. "You mean you really aren't going to go back to Cannon?"

His body stiffened. "Obviously I underestimated the strength of your misgivings. There's only one thing I want to hear, and so help me, you're not able to tell me, so let's not prolong this." His voice grated.

"Since I'll be leaving Gardiner in the

morning, I'll say goodbye now and let myself out." He headed for the entrance.

"Jarod—"

His tall, powerful body kept on walking right out the door into the chilly night. She listened for his footsteps until they faded. Tomorrow he'd be gone and she'd never see him again. By the time she heard his car drive off, she was frantic.

During their long, painful separation, the knowledge that Jarod was in that safe place in Cannon where she could always find him and know he was there serving the parish had sustained her.

But by leaving the priesthood, he'd become a free agent to roam at will wherever he wanted. With whomever he wanted.

She let out an anguished cry.

If she thought this last year had been unbearable without him, she couldn't imagine what the rest of her life would be like not knowing where to find him.

He'd said he would meet a woman who wanted the same things out of life he wanted.

A tremor shook her body.

Sydney was that woman!

Without him, there would be no life for her,

only pain. If she married him and he broke her heart later, could it be any worse than the way she was feeling right now? Probably it would be so much worse, she couldn't abide the thought. But all she knew right now was that she loved him beyond caution or reason. She had to take the risk, if it wasn't too late!

What if he changed his mind and left town tonight? Terrified over the possibility, she found her purse and flew out the front door to her car.

He'd said he was staying at the Firehole Lodge. But when she reached it, she couldn't see his rental car in any of the parking areas.

Where had he gone?

Maybe he'd checked out before he'd come over to the school earlier. If that was true...

She jumped out of her car and dashed inside the lobby. The clerk at the front desk observed her approach with a look of male admiration.

"May I help you?"

"Yes." She swallowed hard. "I'm here to see Mr. Jarod Kendall. Do you know if he's still registered?"

"I'll check."

"Please hurry."

"Sounds like it's a matter of life and death," he teased.

"It is," she answered soberly.

If I can't find him, then I might as well be dead.

"I have good news. He hasn't checked out yet."

"Thank heaven. I didn't see his car, but would you mind ringing his room anyway?"

He nodded before doing her bidding. After a minute he hung up. "Sorry. He's not answering."

"Could you tell me what room he's in?"

He grinned. "I shouldn't, but I will. Number 25. The entrance for that part of the building is in back."

"Thank you."

"No problem."

She hurried outside and drove her car around where she could see his when he returned. But it was after midnight and all the parking spaces were taken. Since it was the beginning of the long Labor Day weekend, she wasn't surprised to see so many last-minute vacationers.

Where was Jarod?

Finally she found one empty spot at the far end and pulled into it. While she waited for him, she turned on the heater. No telling where he'd gone. If he'd taken a drive, he might not return for hours.

Just when she thought he wasn't going to come, she saw headlights and watched him pull into his designated spot near the entrance. Like quicksilver, he got out of his car and went inside the building, too fast for her to catch up to him.

She raced from her car to follow him. Just before he disappeared inside his room, she called his name. But by this time she was so out of breath, she wasn't certain he even heard her.

"Jarod?" she cried again outside his door.

Suddenly it opened.

In the orange light of the hallway, she saw his broad chest rise and fall as if he were sustaining a great shock.

Wordlessly, he reached for her.

CHAPTER FIVE

SUDDENLY Sydney found herself backed up against the inside wall, pinned there by Jarod's hard-muscled body. His hands were braced on either side of her head as he leaned into her. Only a few centimeters separated their mouths.

"Though you can't say the words yet, you wouldn't be here if your answer weren't yes. Kiss me, Sydney."

Moaning her compliance, she obeyed her own overpowering instinct to meet the compelling urgency of his entreaty. At the first fusion of their lips, the world swirled around her, driving her to cling to him. He was the breath of life to her.

Nothing had prepared her for this explosion of hunger or the ecstasy he created. There was a refined savagery in the way he was holding and kissing her.

Delirious with the passion born of their suppressed desire, they drank longer and deeper from each other's mouths until she felt white-hot heat start to devour her. It spread from the secret core of her body to radiate to her very fingertips.

His moans followed hers as they gave and took indescribable pleasure from each other in the dark confines of the room.

"I love you, I love you," she cried rapturously while her lips traveled the contours of his unforgettable male face. "You're such a beautiful man, I'm in awe," she whispered into the luxuriant black hair she couldn't stop touching.

She felt him suck in his breath. He kissed the base of her throat where her pulse throbbed. "I don't dare tell you how I feel about you or else I will really start to show you, and I can't do that until I have your parents' permission to marry you."

Very gently, he disengaged himself until she stood there alone, swaying and bereft.

After emerging from a fiery furnace where she wanted to stay and be consumed by the flames, the mention of her family acted like a numbing cascade of glacier water. It effectively put out the fire he'd generated, robbing her of the inexplicable joy she'd just experienced in his strong arms.

She turned her body away from him and clung to the wall. "They'll never give it. I'll quit my job and we can be married in Europe."

Sydney couldn't believe she'd just said that, but her love for Jarod was too great for it to be jeopardized now.

Jarod was still so close to her, she could feel the heat from his body. "I won't marry you without at least giving them a chance first. Your parents brought you into this world. You're their only child. They adore you.

"Do you honestly believe you and I could take full joy in our union if they weren't behind it, anxious to be a part of it? If my own family's miserable failures did nothing else, they taught me how precious and sacred those ties are.

"I haven't given up on my family yet, Sydney, and I refuse to start out married life with you estranged from your parents. It won't work. We'd both be desperately unhappy—unable to build a life that's going to last."

White-faced, she turned to him. "You don't know them the way I do. To marry a man outside their church would be incomprehensible to them. Especially one w-wh—"

"Who's an ex-priest?" he broke in. His lips twitched. Any hint of a smile made him so gorgeous, she got lost just staring at him. "Maybe that will work in my favor."

"Don't tease about something this earthshaking—" she begged him.

"*Sydney*—"

He pulled her back in his arms. She burrowed against his solid shoulder while he rocked her in place. "Our love has brought us this far. It's going to take us all the way.

"Since you don't have to be back to school until Monday, let's fly to Bismarck tomorrow morning and pay them a surprise visit."

In anyone else's case, his suggestion would have made perfect sense, but Jarod had no idea what he'd be up against with her parents. A frightened tremor shook her body.

He buried his face in the gold satin of her hair. "When you tremble like this, I want to take you to bed and make you forget everything and everyone else but me. Soon that's exactly what I'm going to do.

"But for now, you have to leave my room.

Otherwise I won't be responsible for my actions, and then you'll have something else to feel guilty about."

She groaned, knowing he was right, but her reaction was to press herself harder against him. "I don't want to move from your arms. Not ever again."

"After we receive your parents' blessing, I swear I'll never let you out of my sight." He took her mouth in another long, hard kiss, then abruptly tore his lips from hers.

"Come on. I'll walk you to your car and follow you home so I know you get in your apartment safely."

She gazed up at him with her heart in her eyes. "I wish—"

"So do I." He read her mind with unerring accuracy. "But it wouldn't be a good idea to spend the night at your place. I wouldn't last two minutes on your couch before I came in your bedroom and joined you. So I'll pick you up at six in the morning and we'll have breakfast on our way to the airport."

Six in the morning.

As he walked her to her car, Sydney didn't know if she could make it through the night without him—now that they were finally together again. Right now he was being the strong one. The discipline of a priest made him exceptional…yet she wished that for this one time, he'd give in to his human side.

After he'd helped her in the car, he took another sensuous kiss from her mouth.

"I'm aware of what you're thinking, but you're wrong about me. I'm more human than you know. One more hurdle, then you're going to find out what it's like to be loved by a man."

"Rick? Did I wake you?"

"You know better than that."

"It's still early, but this news can't wait."

"Then my prayers have been answered."

"Almost. We're at the Bismarck airport waiting for a taxi. I'm about to meet Sydney's parents. Depending on how things go, I'd like her to meet you and Kay. Is your schedule flexible enough for you to drive over from Cannon tomorrow and meet us here for dinner?"

"I'll fix it so it is."

"Good. I'll call you in the morning and let you know the exact time and place."

"Jarod?"

"Yes?"

"You sound different. The happiness in your voice—" Rick couldn't go on, he was struggling to stay in control.

Jarod discovered he had to clear his own throat. "Only a happily married man like you would know how I'm feeling right now."

The taxi had pulled up to the curb.

"Thanks for being there, Rick."

He hung up and turned to Sydney who was looking too anxious and frightened on this incredible day of days. "They'll join us tomorrow evening."

Taking her arm, he helped her into the back of the cab and shut the door. Sydney gave the driver directions to her parents' ranch house, then clung to Jarod's side.

She was trembling again, this time out of pure fear.

As Jarod had learned early in life, for good or bad, the power of family was the greatest force there was. He held her tighter.

Finally she sat up straight. "I—I'd better phone my parents and tell them I'm about to arrive with someone."

Jarod had wondered when she'd get around to it. It worried him she'd taken this long to find the courage.

"This is wonderful, honey. Your mom was just saying how upset she was that you wouldn't be here for the holiday. She's going to be thrilled when she comes back from the store and finds you here."

"Dad?" Sydney's voice caught. "Before we hang up you need to know I'm bringing someone with me."

"One of your girlfriends from the Park?"

She gripped her cell phone tighter. "No. It's a man."

Silence greeted her ears before he said, "Well, this *is* news."

Oh Dad— If you only knew—

The dynamics in the Taylor household didn't work the same way they did in some families. Inviting a man home to dinner, let alone to be an overnight guest, meant something of extraordinary significance had happened.

Sydney knew instinctively you didn't take that final step unless you wanted the family to assume this was the man you were going to marry.

Jarod Kendall had only made it over her

parents' threshold in her dreams. All of them had turned into nightmares because he'd come dressed in his priestly vestments. Such wouldn't be the case if Sydney had fallen in love with a local from Bismarck who attended her parents' church. They could approve wholeheartedly of someone like that, a man they could relate to spiritually, who had no baggage.

Someone nice and uncomplicated. Someone there'd be nothing not to like. A rancher who would charm her mom by complimenting her cooking. A man who was open, with an easy-to-get-to-know nature her dad could admire. A man like Joe, her cousin's husband.

Sydney's parents liked him a lot. He was the solid, reliable type who would be a devoted husband and father. Joe had proved to be a hard worker who could talk ranching and horses with the other men.

If Sydney had fallen for a man like that, nothing would be standing in the way of her happiness.

"How long will you be staying?" her father asked, jolting her from the fears that had been plaguing her all night so she'd had no sleep.

"That depends…on a lot of things."

"I see."

"We'll be there in a minute, Dad."

"Can't wait."

But he hadn't said it with the same intensity as before. He knew without her telling him that something was wrong. Something big.

Huge.

"It's going to be all right," Jarod whispered after she hung up. He kissed her neck before claiming her mouth once more.

Forgetting the driver, she kissed him back with a ferocity that would shock her when she thought about it later.

Not until the cab slowed to a stop did Sydney realize they'd arrived at the house. With her cheeks on fire, she pulled away from Jarod and slid out her side of the car before he could come around to help her.

Relieved her father wasn't out on the porch watching for them, she waited on the steps for Jarod who paid the driver before he pulled their overnight bags from the trunk.

To see the man she loved come walking toward her family home in broad daylight still made her feel like she was in the middle of some impossible dream.

He was dressed in the tan suit he'd worn the

other day. The dazzling white shirt gave him a sophistication her parents would immediately notice.

Her dad was medium-size. Nothing like Jarod whose powerful build and height could be intimidating to some men less sure of themselves.

But it wasn't the physical that mattered as much in her parents' eyes. They took measure of other things more important...

One thing that was the *most* important.

She felt Jarod slide his hand up her back to her neck and cup it. "Ready?"

"No," she answered honestly.

"Courage, my love."

My love.

He was *her* love. Her parents had to accept him. *They had to!*

Taking the final step, she opened the door. "Mom? Dad? We're here!"

"Your mother just got home. Come on in the living room, honey."

Jarod followed her into the house and shut the door before lowering the bags. She took his arm and they walked through the foyer. Her parents were already on their way to greet them.

Sydney saw the way their gazes summed up

Jarod without being obvious. He was by far and away the most handsome, impressive-looking man they'd ever met or could hope to meet.

After hugging both of them she said, "Mom and Dad, I'd like you to meet Jarod Kendall."

She turned to the man who'd set her on fire from the first moment she'd met him. He stood a few feet away, urbane and confident. "Jarod? This is my mother, Margaret, and my father, Wayne."

Jarod extended his hand for the two of them to shake. "How do you do?" Flashing a white smile he said, "It's a real pleasure to meet Sydney's family at last."

Those words caused her parents' eyes to meet before giving Jarod a second and third glance.

"Why don't we all sit down?" Sydney suggested nervously. She was ready to jump out of her skin. When Jarod took a place on the couch, she sat next to him.

"Can I get either of you something to eat?" her mother asked, always concerned for everyone's comfort. It was one of the many Midwestern traits Sydney loved about her parents.

"We ate on the plane, Mom. But maybe you want something?" She turned to Jarod.

"Not right now, but thank you anyway, Mrs. Taylor."

Her father sat forward in his easy chair with his hands folded between his legs. "So, Jarod. Are you a park ranger?"

"No—" Sydney blurted. "Jarod's the man I met in Cannon while I was teaching school."

The mention of Cannon acted like a bomb going off. Suddenly there was tension in the living room as Sydney had known there would be. Only a few days ago her parents had vetted her about the mystery man from her past. Now he was here in their home.

"He came to see me in Gardiner." She moaned inwardly because there was no easy way to impart certain facts that were going to come as a stunning shock. All she could do was plunge ahead. Swallowing hard she said, "Jarod's asked me to marry him, and I've said yes."

Sounds of surprise came out of her parents. Not happy, not unhappy.

"We'd like your blessing, but I realize we've sprung this on you without any advance warning," Jarod interjected with a calm Sydney would kill to possess. "Since she has this time off from her teaching, we thought we'd take advantage of the holiday for all of us to meet and get acquainted."

"Well now." Her father spoke first. "We knew Sydney was in love with someone back in Cannon. I guess what Margaret and I don't understand is why it has taken until today for a meeting to take place."

"Are you a teacher?" her mother inquired. "Is that how you and our daughter met?"

Sydney was shaking so hard Jarod must have felt it because he reached out and caught hold of her hand.

"Actually I met Sydney when she brought one of her high school students to my office for counseling."

"Then you work for the public schools?" her mother persisted.

"No." Jarod let Sydney's hand go and got to his feet. "I'm originally from Long Island, New York. My family still lives there. I have a brother Drew, and a sister Liz.

"After graduating from Yale, I joined the Catholic church, then attended ministerial school in St. Paul, Minnesota, and became a priest. That was ten years ago. Until approximately two months ago, I served as the parish priest in Cannon."

Her mother sat there frozen-faced. "I thought priests couldn't marry," she clipped out sternly.

Sydney's father looked nonplussed. "Does that mean your assignment has been changed?"

At this juncture Sydney bowed her head, waiting for the moment of truth.

"I know this is difficult, but I'll try and answer your questions. When I discovered that my love for Sydney would never go away, I laid my case before the bishop. Less than a week ago, I left the priesthood. I don't have the Pope's sanction. Possibly I never will. But God understands this was something I had to do."

"Excuse me for a moment."

As her mother left the room, Sydney sent Jarod a signal before jumping up to follow her into the kitchen.

"Mom?" Her mother started getting food out of the fridge to make sandwiches. "Stop for a minute and look at me."

Her parent kept working.

"I swear we didn't have an affair, Mom. The only person who behaved dishonorably was *me*.

Jarod never did one thing to encourage me. He never sought me out."

Finally her mother glanced up at her. "But he didn't ask you not to come, did he?"

After a slight hesitation, "No."

"Then you were both at fault. If you want my blessing, I can't in good faith give it to you. Different backgrounds and pasts bring on their own problems, and marriage is hard enough.

"By marrying this man, you're taking on more than a husband. He might have physically left the priesthood, but the church inside him hasn't left. I don't care what he believes or what you want to believe, it will always have a stranglehold on him. Probably not so noticeably at first.

"Wait until the children come."

"No, Mom, we haven't discussed any of that yet."

"Of course not. You're too much in love to see the dangers ahead. I have eyes in my head. I can see why your physical attraction to him is so strong. Besides his exceptional looks, he's intelligent, well educated. But in a spiritual sense he's been married to the priesthood for a long time. Part of him will never be able to give it up.

"When you discover you need him most, he

may not be there for you the way you want. I'm not trying to say hurtful things to you, Sydney. I love you, honey, but what you're planning to do could come back to bite you. Since I'm your mother, I feel I have to warn you of these things before it's too late."

"It's already too late," Sydney whispered. "For two years I've been searching my heart for answers. It came when he showed up at my door the other night. I've worried about all of those things, but I love Jarod. We want to be married right away."

"Where will the ceremony take place?"

"I don't know yet. Jarod wanted to meet you before we talked about anything else. He's such a wonderful man, Mom."

"I'm sure he is. Otherwise you wouldn't be head over heels in love with him. But he doesn't have a spiritual home right now. Neither do you. Think upon that, Sydney."

"That's all I've done."

Her mother picked up the sandwich platter and headed out the door. Sydney grabbed the paper plates and napkins plus the bowl of chips before following her.

The second she entered the living room, she

noticed Jarod sitting on a chair next to her father. They were in deep discussion. Judging by her father's demeanor, he wasn't any happier about the situation than her mother.

After going back for sodas, she served everyone one, then sat down on the couch. Her father looked at her in pain before shaking his head.

"You're a twenty-eight-year-old woman, capable of running your own life and managing your affairs. If you and Jarod are intent on marrying, then there's nothing Margaret and I can say.

"I've told Jarod my concerns, so we have an understanding. When you were a baby, I have to admit this state of affairs wasn't what I had in mind for you."

Tears trembled on the edges of her eyelashes. She jumped up abruptly. "I knew it was going to be like this, but can't you and Mom be just a little bit happy for us? Can't you give us one encouraging smile for good luck? No matter how strong and noble Jarod is, this couldn't be easy for him!"

"We know that, honey, and we respect him for the respect he has shown us. But when two people talk of marriage in your circumstances, it's precarious at best.

"If you haven't considered that people who knew Jarod before might ostracize him for what he's done, then I have."

Her mother nodded. "Your dad's right, Sydney. When he's the object of ridicule, you'll feel the effect, too. If there's a chance of making this work, then you'd be wise to move where no one knows either of you. That way you can begin your life together with the least amount of turmoil."

Sydney struggled to stay composed. "Jarod mentioned Europe. Would that be far enough away for you?" she cried before turning to Jarod. "Let's go, Jarod."

He remained in place. "Not yet. There are a few more things I'd like to say to your parents."

She couldn't imagine what was in his mind, but some inexplicable force was driving him. She had the feeling she couldn't have dissuaded him for any reason.

While her parents eyed him with wooden expressions, Sydney sat down beside him once more. She had no idea what he was about to say. She couldn't imagine there being anything else *to* say.

It pained her that her parents remained so quiet and aloof. Though she'd warned him, she was still wounded by their behavior, and she hurt for him. He was the man she was going to marry!

Jarod sat forward to address them. "When I asked Sydney to be my wife, I didn't know what her answer would be. I told her that if she said no, I planned to live and work abroad. But that wouldn't have been my first choice.

"In the last ten years I've learned to love North Dakota. It's been my home for so long, I'm loathe to leave it. During the talks in my office when Sydney accompanied Brenda, I learned how much she loves it here, too. I envied her such a happy childhood riding horses and helping you on the ranch. It sounded like the perfect life."

Sydney had no idea these were his feelings.

"The last thing I want to do is take her away from her family and people she's known for a lifetime. What I'd really like to do is buy some property around here and build a house for us."

"You're kidding—"

His head swerved toward her. There was fire in his eye.

"You're not kidding—" she muttered in shock.

"Not at all."

"But how would you earn a living?"

"I've got it all planned…"

CHAPTER SIX

SYDNEY SHOOK her head. "You're not making sense."

"If my counseling project doesn't work out, I have another plan. About five years ago I purchased a tract of land for the parish and rallied some of the men so we could grow garlic bulbs. From the revenue produced, we were able to build a new gym for the youth center."

"Garlic you say?" her father interjected, reminding Sydney her parents were still in the room. Obviously Jarod had captured his interest.

"Yes. The hearty kind to withstand the low winter temperatures here. It was an experiment that became successful."

"I didn't know that," Sydney broke in.

The corner of Jarod's sensual mouth lifted in a subtle smile that turned her heart over. "There are a lot of things we don't know about each other, but we will. And one thing is certain, taking you away from your parents won't make any of us happy. I'm living proof that an ugly, estranged family situation can result in devastating consequences."

"That's very true," her mother concurred, but it sounded too self-righteous to Sydney's ears.

Oh, Mom. Why can't you unbend?

He turned to them again. "Because I was a priest, there's every chance that someone is going to recognize me and either remain friends, or as you suggested, turn their back on me. But that could happen anywhere since I'm not about to lie concerning my activities after college.

"Being a priest represented the happiest time in my life. As I found out after meeting Sydney, there's only one thing more to add to that happiness. It's marriage and children to the woman I love.

"I haven't left the Church. There will be times when I go to worship just as you go to your church to do the same thing. Whether Sydney accompanies me or not is strictly her choice. If and when children come to our marriage, I want them to attend church. It doesn't matter which one.

"In my years of counseling couples, I've learned that two parents who take their children to the same church provide a solid base that builds confidence and security. Sydney and I will have to agree on that. If she wants to raise her children in your local church I'll attend with her, and still go to my own privately.

"But in order to get our marriage off to the very best start, I was hoping we could be married in your home, surrounded by your extended family and friends."

It'll never happen, Jarod. Not in a hundred years.

"I'll invite my family of course, but it's anyone's guess if they'll come."

"Why is that?" her mother asked after exchanging a silent glance with Sydney's father.

"Because my becoming a priest was something they couldn't comprehend or condone any more than you do. My mother still sends me a card on birthdays and at Christmas. My brother and sister phone occasionally."

Sydney slid off the couch. "What about your father?"

"I write my parents every month, but he's

never written back. I haven't heard from him in ten years."

A pained cry poured from Sydney's throat. "That's horrible."

Shadows darkened his eyes. "It's been my reality. But I don't want it to be yours."

She shivered because Jarod might as well have said, *I won't let it be ours*. Still holding her gaze he said, "If our marriage is going to tear you and your family apart, then we have to be prepared for a lot of heartache."

Upon that remark he stood up. "What I'm going to do is leave you here to spend the night. I'll go back to the hotel, and we'll talk again in the morning."

"No, Jarod. I'm coming with you!" It hit her again just how much he'd given up to be with her. She was afraid for them to be apart for any reason, but right now wasn't the time for her to analyze what was at the bottom of those fears.

"Jarod's right, Sydney. We need time to talk alone. I'll walk you to the door."

Jarod moved closer to kiss her cheek. His eyes sent her the clear message that this separation was going to be agony for him, too. "Call me later on my cell," he whispered.

She nodded, having to hold back from throwing her arms around him and never letting go.

When the two men left the room her mother flashed her a questioning glance. "Where does an ex-priest get money to buy land and a house?"

Oh, Mom.

"Come in the kitchen and I'll explain."

She hurried ahead and opened the flour bin drawer. Her mother looked totally perplexed when Sydney lifted out the ten-pound sack.

"See the brand?"

The second her mother put two and two together, she stared at Sydney in fresh alarm, but for once she didn't say anything.

To Sydney's parents, Jarod came from a background and had lived a life so foreign to everything they knew, they were having trouble absorbing it all, especially her mother.

"Take away the trappings, Mom, and you can see he's a marvelous human being."

Her mother got that set expression on her face. "I'll admit he's the most forthright man I ever met."

"He's more than that!" Sydney cried in frustration.

A strange sound came out of her mother. "Yes. He has you under his spell. I'm afraid for you, Sydney. This man has the power to destroy you."

Behind her mother's intransigence, Sydney detected real anxiety. In all honesty, she couldn't deny her own deep-seated fears that the day could come when marriage might not be the ultimate answer for Jarod. He might want to break his vows to her, too.

She didn't want to think about it or believe it could happen, but with his history, she had to at least acknowledge the possibility.

"I'm scared, too, Mom. But I'm more scared of letting him go and never seeing him again."

"I know."

Her mother turned away and left the kitchen.

Jarod grazed the TV channels. Nothing held his interest. Nothing could have captured his attention while he was waiting to hear from Sydney.

For the last ten years he'd lived and worked among Midwesterners, but he had to admit her parents displayed an insular quality that was pretty well impossible to penetrate.

Their quiet, disapproving stoicism explained

the depth of her guilt. Nothing could be more intimidating to a child growing up than to read the censure in her parents' eyes or tone of voice.

He didn't know what was worse. The ear-splitting battles his own parents waged for everyone in the household to hear, or the crushing silence from two parents whose demeanor would put off the most courageous of their children.

Considering the life she'd come from, Sydney was the most unique, courageous woman he knew to be willing to take him on. But he'd be a fool to rule out the possibility that her parents' arguments against marrying him had taken hold.

The mere thought of a life without her caused him to break out in a cold sweat.

By eleven, he couldn't lie there any longer and levered himself from the bed to take a shower. When he reentered the room, he saw the blue light flashing from the cell he'd left on the bedside table.

Sydney? Only a handful of people knew his number.

In a few swift strides he crossed the room and checked the caller ID before phoning her back.

"Jarod?" she answered breathlessly after the first ring. "I've been trying to reach you. Where have you been?"

If he didn't know better, he would think she was angry. But that was stark staring fear he'd heard in her voice just now. His black brows met in a frown.

"I waited all evening for your call, then took a shower."

After a palpable silence. "You've been there the whole time?"

"Where would I go without you?"

"I—I don't know," she dissembled.

His thoughts flew. He couldn't let this pass. "Sydney? If we don't have total honesty between us, we have nothing. Tell me what got you so worried." He thought he knew, but he needed to hear her say it.

"You can't deny that you have friends at the diocese here in Bismarck." Her voice trembled as she said the words.

He unconsciously rubbed his thumb over his lower lip. "That's true. There'll be times in the future when I'll want to see them, but you'll always know about it first. That's a promise I'll make to you right now."

An anguished cry met his ears. "You don't have to promise me anything! A marriage starting out with promises no one should be held to wouldn't last two minutes."

Agreed.

Shifting his weight he said, "Everything okay?"

"Nothing's changed. Will you please come and get me now?"

He sucked in his breath. "I'll be there in ten minutes."

"I'll wait on the porch for you."

After the way her parents had treated Jarod, Sydney reeled from pain she'd never get over. With them in bed, she tiptoed through the house and let herself out the front door to wait.

The second she saw his rental car and climbed in the passenger side, he pulled her into his arms, covering her wet face with kisses.

"Give them time, Sydney. For ten years I've worked with people exactly like your parents. They may be a different religion, but deep down inside we're all the same. What they want is your happiness."

Even if what he said was true, she was too convulsed to speak. Finally she raised her head to give him room enough to drive. "I'm sorry," she half gasped when she realized she'd wet the front of his shirt and jacket.

"Shh." He leaned across to silence her with his lips once more. "I've got you in my arms. It's all that matters."

She turned her face into his neck. "They didn't even ask about your family. Nothing!"

"It's human nature to fight for your own. Forgive them, Sydney."

"I don't know if I can."

After that remark, Jarod backed out of the driveway and they headed for town. "Marriage is one of the ceremonies celebrated by every group of people on earth. It's the high point, something your parents have been waiting for, dreaming about. Today they were confronted by a reality they weren't prepared for.

"But since you're living proof they raised a wonderful daughter, I have to believe that one day they'll recover and embrace our marriage."

"You have more faith than I do."

"They're not my parents," he murmured dryly.

She gazed over at him through tremulous eyes. "When am I going to meet your mother and father?"

"If they don't fly out for our wedding, then we'll fly there at the first opportunity."

A shiver chased across her skin. "Something's horribly wrong when our own families can't break down long enough to celebrate with us."

"I know two people who will," he assured her. "Rick said he'd be my best man. We talked on the phone earlier. He and Kay were going to join us for dinner tomorrow night, but some unexpected church business came up so you'll have to meet them later."

"I'd like that. My friend Gilly will be back from her honeymoon next week. She was the one person I could confide in about you. When she finds out we're together, she'll be overjoyed. I know she and Alex will want to be witnesses."

"That's good. I'm looking forward to meeting her."

"Alex is wonderful, too. He's the head of the Volcano Observatory at Yellowstone Park. I've a feeling you and he will really hit it off."

"What's he like?"

"He lights his own fires, just like you."

"Is that so." He reached for her hand and kissed her palm, sending darts of awareness through her body.

"Yes, it is," she came back slightly out of breath from his touch. "Jarod? Since you haven't started that counseling job yet, do you want me to break my teaching contract so we can go to Europe? Please tell me the truth."

"I only mentioned it in case you couldn't bring yourself to marry me." He gripped her hand tighter. "But now that I know we're going to have a life together, Gardiner sounds like an ideal place for us to start out. I love the area, but that's because you're in it."

Thrilled by his words, she kissed his finger-tips. "I can't wait till we get back. You can move into my apartment."

"You mean after we're married."

"No. I mean tomorrow." Her voice throbbed. "I couldn't stay away from you now."

He pulled into a parking space at their hotel and shut off the motor, then turned to look at her through veiled eyes.

"You've never been intimate with a man, have you?"

Her cheeks filled with warmth. "No."

He drew in a deep breath. "I didn't think so."

"Not so much because of any rules, but

because you're the only man I've ever truly desired heart and soul."

"That's the way it should be." His jaw hardened. "I'm sorry to say that in the past, I broke some rules to be with women I had no intention of marrying. But when I became a priest, I began a new life.

"And now I'm a different man it wouldn't be possible for me to move in with you and not make love to you. Since you've waited this long, then I want to honor you, so I'm going to stay at the Firehole Lodge until we're married."

"No, Jarod. I don't want to live alone any longer."

"Neither do I." His voice grated. "Since you left Cannon, I've had dreams about you, about holding you in my arms on cold winter nights and warm summer mornings. But I can wait a few more weeks for my prize."

Struggling against his reasoning she cried, "I don't think I can—"

"Don't forget the word will spread you're marrying an ex-priest. I'm already damned in some people's eyes. Living with you before I'm your husband will add fuel to that particular fire. You know I'm right."

Yes. She knew.

"That's why we're going to sleep in separate rooms tonight and every night until you become Mrs. Jarod Kendall. Which reminds me we need to see about a ring for you before we leave Bismarck in the morning."

She shook her head. "I don't need one. It isn't important."

"But I need to give you one. It's something I've been looking forward to doing. You have to understand this whole experience is one I willingly gave up before I met you. Now everything is changed."

Another tremor shook her body. He sounded happy now. But what if married life didn't live up to his expectations? What if her parents were right?

"How about a solitaire?" The jeweler picked up another diamond ring with a white-gold setting.

"Let's see how it looks on your finger."

Before the jeweler could do the honors, Jarod reached for her hand and slid it onto her ring finger. It was the perfect size.

"Do you like it?"

Sydney felt Jarod's eyes on her. Their green

brilliance rivaled the dazzling one-carat stone. She could tell he wanted her to pick this one. It happened to be her favorite, too.

"I love it!"

"Then that's it." He looked at the jeweler. "Now we'd like to see some wedding rings. My fiancée has beautiful hands. I think a wide gold band."

His compliments at odd moments, so unexpected and genuine, thrilled her as nothing else could. All the time he'd been a priest, he'd noticed little things about her, but she hadn't been aware of his private thoughts. To be with him like this and share everything in the open like a normal couple was a revelation.

Once they'd decided on her ring, she asked him to bring out some men's wedding rings. "I'd like one with a stone the same color as Jarod's eyes."

The jeweler nodded. "I noticed them right away. Just a moment. Something came in from Hong Kong I want you to see."

While he went over to one of his drawers, Jarod slid his hands to her shoulders from behind. "I'd be happy with a simple band."

"You wore one like that when you were a priest. I want this to be different. Every time you look at it, I want it to remind you that when I fell in love with you, I fell in love with everything about you, especially your eyes."

He didn't say anything, only buried his face in the gold silk of her hair.

Seconds later, the jeweler returned. "What do you think?"

It was a deep-set, square stone in a wide, dark gold band. "I adore it!" Sydney cried. She turned to Jarod. "Put it on."

Slowly he did her bidding.

"It's perfect, and it fits!" she announced to the jeweler. "We'll take it."

A smile hovered around Jarod's lips as he pulled out his credit card. But when the jeweler started to add up the bill, Sydney took a card from her wallet, too.

Jarod frowned, but she cupped the side of his arresting face with her hand. "Your ring is my gift. I've waited years to buy one for the man I love. You wouldn't deny me that pleasure, would you?"

In a few minutes they left the shop with their purchases. The excitement of walking to the car wearing her new engagement ring made her positively euphoric. When they got inside, she threw her arms around his neck. Despite people walking by, she covered his face with kisses.

"I love you so much, it hurts."

He devoured her mouth until she was witless. When he finally tore his lips from hers, she groaned in protest.

"As soon as we're married, I'm going to take all our pain away. That's one promise I can make and know I'll keep it. But right now we have a plane to catch, and I need to get the rental car back first."

"I—I didn't know it was getting so late." Sydney moved far enough away from him so he could maneuver the car.

Once they reached the airport and returned the car, Jarod ushered her to the counter to check in their bags. When the female employee lifted her head, Sydney saw recognition flicker in the other woman's eyes. She darted a brief glance to Sydney before her attention refastened on Jarod.

"Father Kendall? I thought it was you!"

"Good morning, Sally."

Sydney hurriedly stood behind him. A line had formed behind her. She noticed the way the thirtyish-looking employee was so busy staring at Jarod, she almost forgot to check him in.

After handing him his boarding pass she said, "Someone at the diocese said you've been on retreat. You look…wonderful."

"I feel wonderful."

"Between you and me, I like you without a beard." She bantered easily with him. "How does it feel?"

"Liberating."

"What a surprise everyone in Cannon is going to have next Sunday."

"I'm afraid I won't be there."

"Extending your vacation a while longer?"

"Something like that."

Their conversation prompted Sydney to stand a little more apart from him so the other woman wouldn't associate them being together.

"Heaven knows you work so hard you deserve more time off than they give you. Enjoy the rest of your holiday."

"Will do."

Instead of walking on, he moved to the side so Sydney could check in. Once she had her boarding pass in hand, she started for the gate, trying to get ahead of Jarod so people would assume she was alone.

But he was having none of that. Before

they'd reached the crowd of people waiting to board, he put his arm around her shoulders, pulling her close.

"I know what you were thinking back there, but you'd be wrong. Let's get one thing clear. The only reason I didn't introduce you to Sally and explain myself was because other people were waiting to be checked through. She works part-time at the diocese answering the phone, and will learn the truth soon enough.

"You could have no comprehension of what it means to me to be an engaged man. I'm living for the moment we're married, Sydney. There isn't a male in sight who hasn't noticed you and wouldn't sell his soul for the right to be in my place. It's all I can do not to shout to everyone that you're mine," he claimed in a fierce tone.

"Jarod—"

"It's true and you know it."

Keep telling me those things, my darling. I want to believe you.

Three hours later, Jarod followed Sydney into her apartment and put her bag down in the living room. At last they were alone and turned instinctively to each other, not needing words.

Like a man dying of thirst, he crushed her against him and drank from her mouth. Now that he had the right to communicate with her in the most elemental of ways, he realized she'd become his addiction.

All he wanted was to cling to her. Being able to touch her, to bury his face in her scented neck and hair was so intoxicating, he feared he might break his own rule after all.

"Help me, Sydney. Tell me to leave."

Her answer was to mold herself to him until their mouths and bodies crossed that seamless line into forgetfulness.

He rubbed his hands over her back. "When you were in Cannon, do you have any idea how many times I imagined being together with you like this?"

She took a shaky breath. "Yes. I lived for every precious moment I could steal in order to see you for even a few minutes in passing. Talk about torture."

"I know." He clasped her tighter.

"Brenda never betrayed herself, but she was a smart girl and knew how I felt about you, Jarod. I know that's why she pretended she didn't have the courage to attend her counseling sessions without me along."

His lips roved over her upturned features. She was such a gorgeous woman, he couldn't get enough of her. "I'm afraid neither of us fooled Brenda. When I didn't tell her I needed to see her alone, she never questioned it."

"You worked wonders with her."

"So did you, Sydney. That entry in her journal was a plea for help, and you picked up on it as she hoped you would. The last time I ever saw her, she said she wished you and I were married so we could be her baby's adoptive parents."

"*What?*"

Sydney's throat almost closed up. She tilted her head back so she could see into his eyes.

He brushed his mouth against her. "At the time, Brenda couldn't possibly have known how her comment affected me. I was consumed with thoughts of what it would be like to have children with you. Our own children.

"Sydney? After we're married, do you want to start a family right away?"

She heard his unspoken plea, but he needn't have worried. "Yes! Oh yes!"

An unmistakable gleam of satisfaction caused his eyes to radiate little points of green light.

"My cousin's about ready to give birth to her first child. I'm happy for her, but I've been envious, too, because she and Joe were able to meet and get married without problems."

"In other words, they were surrounded by family and friends when they took their vows in church," Jarod added.

"Yes."

"Your father talked to me about those two."

"Dad approves of Joe, he comes from a ranching background. He fits right in."

"Lucky Joe."

She darted him a pleading glance. "You're the man I'm going to marry so none of it matters—"

"I disagree, Sydney. Though I plan to marry you any way we can, I'd much prefer to do it the old-fashioned way."

"But how can we do that?" Her voice trembled.

"I saw past your parents' guard. If ever two people are grief stricken over what's transpired, they are."

She sobered. "They could have turned everything around with one word of welcome to you."

"Maybe when the shock wears off. For now

you and I have other matters to take care of. I'll run over to the lodge and check back in, then drop by the resort office to let Maureen know I'm ready to start work on Monday. After that, we'll go out for dinner and celebrate our engagement. How does that sound?"

"Like you're not going to be back here soon enough to suit me." She flung her arms around his waist. "Every time you walk out of a door, I'm afraid I won't see you again. I know that sounds paranoid, but I can't help it.

"The other night when I went to the lodge and couldn't find you, I almost went out of my mind. Until the clerk assured me you hadn't checked out, I was afraid you'd decided to just leave Gardiner early.

"Even when he told me you had to be somewhere around, I was terrified I might not see you slip in, and then you'd be gone from me forever."

She tried to fight tears, but they spilled down her face anyway. "I couldn't take it if that happened. Not now."

"Do you think I could?" he demanded emotionally. His hands cupped her face before he kissed her with exquisite tenderness. "I gave up a whole other life for you. I did it of my own free will and volition because you fulfill something in me I could never experience otherwise.

"I know our path won't always be smooth. There will be stormy moments, but I swear before God we'll make it through the good and the bad times because we've found a love too rare to be denied.

"I love you, Sydney. I need you in ways you can't imagine. Don't ever give up on me."

His body strained against her. He was trembling. It filled her with awe the way his vulnerability caused him to cling.

"Oh, darling. As if I could."

He made a sound in his throat. "You used to whisper that endearment to me in my dreams. To hear you say it aloud—to me—"

For this strong, fantastic man to reveal some of his deepest secrets, even for a moment, catapulted her love to achingly new heights.

She wasn't naive. She knew there were other secrets. Maybe he'd share them one day, maybe not.

"Never be afraid to tell me anything, Jarod. The only thing that could hurt us would be for you to hold back."

He grasped her hands. "That works both

ways, Sydney. In our special case, honesty will be the crucial ingredient, no matter what."

Sydney nodded. "No matter what," she repeated against his lips.

His cell phone unexpectedly rang, resounding off the walls of the living room. He kissed the tip of her well-shaped nose before answering it. The caller ID indicated it was Rick.

Jarod clicked on. "You're just the person I wanted to talk to. I'm now an officially engaged man."

"I know."

Rick's comment caused his smile to fade.

Sally—

"The diocese grapevine travels fast."

"She caught the sparkler on your fiancée's finger. That set off fireworks."

Of course.

"I'm glad. It had to come out sometime."

"Where are you?"

"In Gardiner."

"Good."

His one syllable word said it all. The fallout had started. "Thanks for alerting me, Rick. I'll call you later."

Before he'd clicked off, Sydney was right there hugging the life out of him.

Hold on to me, Sydney.

CHAPTER SEVEN

AFTER UNPACKING, Sydney showered before settling down to make some preparations for the first day of class. Incredible to believe that for the rest of her life, she and Jarod would have each other to come home to at the end of the day.

Last weekend she'd been in California in a state of despair, barely functional because the man she loved could never be hers. So much had changed since then, she couldn't relate to that desolate person.

Her gaze rested on the ring he'd pushed home on her finger. The blue-white diamond glinted up at her. He took pleasure in everything to do with their relationship. It shouldn't have surprised her he'd insisted on buying her a ring.

When he'd taken vows of celibacy, he'd rejected the worldly pleasures in order to be a more committed servant. But because the course of his life had taken a dramatic turn to the opposite end of the spectrum, it was only natural that he savored each step along the way.

In that regard, Sydney needed to be sensitive to his wants and moods. He didn't have the same support group anymore. As well as being his companion and lover, she realized she would be his number one fan from here on out.

He'd said he needed her. In his case, it was particularly true. But he would never need her with the same intensity she needed him. She planned to lavish him with so much love, he'd drown in it.

Finding it impossible to concentrate on schoolwork, Sydney left everything on the kitchen table and went into the bedroom to get dressed for dinner.

After changing her mind half a dozen times, she eventually chose to wear her favorite oyster-colored silk blouse with a coffee-toned skirt. At five feet eight, she didn't always wear heels, but she didn't have to worry about being too tall around someone of Jarod's height.

A flick of the brush and a light floral spray was all she needed to feel totally feminine for the incredible man who would become her husband soon.

Trembling with excitement, she paced the floor waiting for him to arrive. After several hours of being apart from him, she discovered she couldn't stand the slightest separation.

When he arrived at her door, he had a distinctive rap that made her smile with pleasure. She raced to open it, and there he was in all his male splendor. With his black hair and those flame-green eyes, the cream-colored sweater and matching chinos provided the perfect foil.

She detected the scent of the soap he'd used in the shower. Mixed with her own fragrance, the combined aroma acted as a special kind of aphrodisiac which increased her desire for him.

Helpless in the face of his overwhelming attraction, she could only murmur his name. No other words would come in her mesmerized state. Her pulse raced from his thorough scrutiny of her face and figure.

"I made reservations at the Moose Lodge dining room, but now that I'm here, I don't want to share you with anyone."

Her breath caught. "I feel the same."

"Stop looking at me that way," he begged. "Otherwise I'm going to have to leave town until the wedding."

"You wouldn't—" she cried, horrified at the very thought, insecurity still nagging at her.

He drew her into his arms and nuzzled her neck. "You know better than that."

She shook her head, still quivering in reaction. "No, I don't."

"I was only teasing you, darling."

Sydney raised anguished eyes to him. "Please don't do that to me yet. This is all too new, and you're too precious to me."

His eyes narrowed on her mouth before he bestowed one wine-dark kiss after another. They caused her to lose all sense of time and place. Jarod had to be the one who held her up when her legs almost gave away.

"I think we need to get married as soon as possible. When I was at the motel, I talked to the pastor. He's free to marry us this coming Saturday or the next. We can get a license tomorrow."

The mention of the clergyman dissipated a little of her euphoria. "If you've contacted him because you think it's what I want, then we need to talk about it because I want what *you* want.

Is there no Catholic priest who would officiate? I'd be willing to do that."

He grasped her shoulders. "I adore you for your unselfishness, but it wouldn't be possible."

"Why? Even if you left the priesthood, you're still a member."

"I'd rather it was someone who will concentrate on you and me, not our religious affiliations."

She stared at him for a long time. Though he'd just shaved, she could detect the faint shadow of his stubble. It made him incredibly appealing.

"Did you ever fantasize about marrying me at the church in Cannon?"

A small nerve throbbed along his jaw. "Yes."

She'd wanted honesty.

"You meant it about taking our children to church."

His chest rose and fell visibly. "Yes," he said again with equal fervor. "Since you accompanied Brenda to Mass on occasion, I assumed you wouldn't have a problem going to a church of our mutual choosing with the children. It's a great place for them to socialize and make friends.

"If I was wrong about that, I need to know how you feel about my taking them."

She couldn't believe they were even having

such a serious conversation. Tonight they were supposed to be celebrating their engagement. But since she'd brought up the subject, she had no right to be upset.

"There's plenty of time for us to talk about this after we're married and have a baby."

He flashed her an enigmatic glance. "That's the time most couples get around to it. But by then emotions are running high. What's upsetting you, Sydney?"

How could she forget Jarod was a counselor by profession, and a superior judge of human nature by virtue of his innate intelligence? On top of that he'd been a priest whom people had sought out to help them resolve domestic disputes.

"Whatever is bothering me is my problem, not yours. I'm so ashamed. Forgive me, Jarod. Let's go to dinner."

He shook his dark head. "Not yet. I'm aware you were raised by two strong-willed parents who were united in their core beliefs. No doubt I've come off sounding too much like them."

Jarod had figured it out a lot sooner than she had.

She averted her eyes. "You're going to wish you'd never met me."

"Don't ever say that again." He crushed her to him. "You have to understand I'm deathly afraid of failing you or any children we might have. I've often thought I had the easier life as a priest. No wife to consult, no children to be a role model for.

"Then I met you and realized I craved the comfort only a woman can bring. Every time I played sports with the kids, I found myself wishing one of them were my own son or daughter. Do you understand what I'm saying?"

She threw her arms around his neck. "Yes, darling. And you're right about children and church. Every child should be so lucky to have two parents who care enough to take them. We'll do it." She kissed his jaw. "Be patient with me. I was an only child. You've got your work cut out."

Rich male laughter suddenly poured out of Jarod. She'd never heard him sound like that before. A subtle transformation was taking place. She loved what was happening with every fiber of her being.

Ten minutes later the hostess at the Moose Lodge dining room showed them to a table next to a bank of picture windows looking out over the pines. The attractive redhead couldn't take her eyes off Jarod.

"Are you a new ranger?" She handed them menus, but her whole focus, like the other females in the room, was caught up in him. No other man in the room had his extraordinary looks or charisma.

"No. My fiancée and I are celebrating our engagement tonight."

The other woman had some difficulty covering her disappointment. "Would you like champagne?"

One of his dark brows lifted. "Sydney?"

"No, thank you."

"It appears neither of us will be having any."

"Then I'll send a waiter over. Enjoy your meal."

"Thank you. We will," Jarod murmured, smiling straight into Sydney's eyes.

"Would you have preferred some wine?" he asked after she'd gone.

"I don't like alcohol of any kind. I got sick on it one time between flights when I was a stewardess. It cured me."

He grasped her hand to examine the diamond in the candlelight. Then he darted her a piercing glance. "I developed an early aversion to it when I came home from high school and found my mother passed out on the bed in the middle of the day.

"She's a beautiful woman. I gct my black hair from her. To see her lying there so hung over she had no idea what time of day it was, and worse, didn't care because my father had been unfaithful to her—something died inside of me."

The waiter chose that moment to bring Chateau-briand for two. When he walked off, Jarod finished talking.

"What I wanted her to do was get up, sober up, and leave him. But she couldn't do it. I thought it was so simple. All she had to do was stop drinking and everything would become clear to her.

"It took years of study at graduate school to understand how complex every human is. Certainly I wasn't capable of fixing their problems or getting her to do something about her alcoholism."

"What a helpless feeling for you, Jarod."

"It was, but if one good thing came out of it, I determined never to drink again. If the tendency truly runs in the genes, I didn't want to take the chance of becoming addicted."

"I can understand that," she commiserated. "I saw a lot of drinking go on in college. Some people can handle it, but those who can't— Well, I'm just thankful that my experience turned me off."

He smiled at her.

"What?" she asked, intrigued.

"The discussions we've been having. The whole time we knew each other in Cannon, we couldn't probe or act too interested."

"Don't remind me," She groaned.

"It's like we're both babies learning new things about each other as fast as we can."

"Thank goodness we aren't!" she cried. "If I had to wait for you to grow up, I'd go mad."

His burst of laughter infected her, making her realize she'd never been so happy in her life.

"Speaking of going mad, what date shall we choose to get married? Next Saturday, or the following one?"

She took a fortifying breath. "I guess I'm hoping that if we put it off one week, it will give someone in your family enough time to consider coming."

"Miracles do happen. Maybe even your parents will have a change of heart and decide to join us."

"By then Gilly and Alex will be back."

"Then it's settled."

She nodded. "Do you think you'll enjoy working at AmeriCore?"

"Yes. It'll be like serving the parish, except that the numbers are bigger. Maureen told me they have 3,000 employees. That translates to a lot of workplace problems. I'm going to feel right at home."

He said it as if he meant it, but Sydney knew it wouldn't be the same for him. After being everyone's spiritual advisor for the last ten years, he was going to miss that special bond.

It made her nervous to think about it, but short of going to Europe as he'd once mentioned, she was grateful this counseling position was available.

"Sydney?" a familiar male voice spoke from behind her chair, jerking her out of her reverie.

She turned her head. "Larry— Hi!"

His eyes glommed onto the diamond on her left hand. He grinned. "It seems you've been holding out on everyone since you resigned. I want an introduction to the man who managed to pull off the impossible."

Gentle laughter escaped her throat. She loved

the big burly ranger. "Larry Smith, meet my fiancé Jarod Kendall. Darling?" Her eyes lit up. "Larry is the chief security officer for the park."

Jarod had gotten to his feet. The two men shook hands, taking stock of each other.

She looked around. "Is your wife with you?"

"Not tonight. I've been in Gardiner on official business with the sheriff. We decided to enjoy a meal."

"If you're not busy now, why don't you join us?" Jarod suggested.

"Maybe for a few minutes. Thanks."

Even if Jarod hadn't liked the ranger right off, he would have issued the invitation. She had to remember her husband-to-be was a people person whose capacity to include everyone made him an outstanding friend and confidant to the people who knew him.

Larry pulled a chair from the other table and made a place for himself. The waiter came by and took his order for coffee. He studied Jarod for a minute.

"You have to be the best kept secret this side of the Continental Divide."

"That's because Sydney only knew me when I was an ordained priest in North Dakota," he stated boldly. "We had no personal relationship until I decided to leave the priesthood to marry her, but she didn't know about it until last week."

Larry digested the news with commendable aplomb. "How long did you serve?"

"Ten years."

He whistled before eyeing her. "The mystery has unfolded."

"What do you mean?"

"No guy could ever get to first base with you. Now I know why." He turned to Jarod. "You're getting the best of the best in Sydney."

His words warmed her heart. "Thank you, Larry."

"I knew it the first time we met." Jarod's voice sounded husky.

"I guess you do if you left for her. Good for you."

Sydney blinked in surprise at his reaction.

"I've been a Catholic all my life, but if you don't mind my saying, I've always felt sorry for the priests."

"I could never mind honesty like that," Jarod commented. "Celibacy is against man's nature, but many of the priests have learned to deal with it. I thought I had until Sydney came along."

Larry smiled at her. "She kind of has that effect on men. Congratulations to both of you. When's the wedding?"

"A week from Saturday."

"Where?"

"At the nondenominational church in Ennis," Sydney supplied.

"Is it going to be a totally private affair?"

She eyed Jarod, silently asking him what he wanted. The answer came when he said, "Sydney and I would be honored if you and your wife would like to attend."

Larry nodded. "We'll be there. What time?"

Excited she said, "I'll phone you and Chief Archer as soon as we've worked out the details. Gilly doesn't even know about it yet, but we'll want her and Alex there, too."

His eyes danced. "Naturally. You two were close." He turned to Jarod. "Ranger King— woops—Ranger Latimer now, is a raving beauty just like Sydney here. It's been hard on all the males around the Park. There'll be mass mourning when the single guys learn she's been nabbed by an outsider."

"I'm that all right."

"I meant no offense."

Jarod smiled broadly. "I know you didn't."

"Well, I'd better get going before my wife starts to worry. It's been a pleasure to meet you, Jarod. After you two get back from your honeymoon, we'd love to throw a party for you. That way you can meet everyone. We have a lot of fun."

Sydney loved him for going out of his way to make Jarod feel welcome. "Thank you so much, Larry."

"I'm looking forward to getting acquainted with all Sydney's friends." Jarod stood up to shake his hand once more.

"Yours sounds like a real love story." His gaze swerved to Sydney. "I'm glad I saw you."

"We are, too," she assured him. Larry didn't know it yet, but he'd just thrown Jarod a lifeline that had helped make a difference already. "Good night."

As soon as he'd gone Jarod said, "Shall we go, too?"

"I'm ready."

After leaving some bills on the table, he helped her up from the chair and they went out to the car. It didn't take long for them to reach the apartment.

"I liked him," he said as they walked inside.

"Larry's one of my favorite people. I don't believe I've ever met anyone more genuine."

"Agreed. He's pretty crazy about you, too." Jarod reached around her waist from behind and pulled her against him.

"I'll bet you drove the little boys wild growing up." His lips brushed the side of her neck, sending delightful ripples through her sensitized body.

She whirled around so she could look at him. "You drive *me* wild. I can't wait to really belong to you."

"I've wanted it longer than you can imagine, which is why I'm going to leave right now."

"You can't!"

"Sydney—" Jarod sounded anguished. "Don't make this any harder on me than it already is."

"Why don't we just hold each other for the rest of the night."

"You honestly think that would work for more than five seconds?"

"We haven't found out yet."

"And you asked me not to tease you," he said in a dry tone.

"I'm not teasing. I'm begging you to stay."

She felt his emotional distance before he released her arms and stepped back. "I can't."

He really meant it. "Why?"

"I made a promise to myself."

"I see."

"I wish I could make you understand."

"Try me."

A deep sigh came out of him. "I want to do everything right. Our love is a sacrament, Sydney. To treat it less than it is would be cheating both of us."

She marveled at the depth of this man. His integrity humbled her. "I wish I were as strong as you."

His eyes glittered with unnamed emotion. "You're wrong. I'm the one with the fatal weakness. Have you forgotten I came to you?"

Leaving her to ponder that question, he disappeared out the door.

Fatal weakness?

If that was how he viewed himself, did it mean he despised that part of his nature?

Because of it, would he end up despising her?

Always at the heart of her newly found happiness lurked the niggling fear Jarod would live to regret his decision. But that was no way to live. Every couple faced challenges in marriage.

Hers was to think positive thoughts and refuse to let the negative take over. Or like her mother had said, it would destroy her.

The bell rang, ending seventh period. All things considered, the first week of school had gone well.

Sydney breathed a sigh of relief as the students filed out of class. In a half hour she planned to meet Jarod to finalize everything with the pastor.

Seven days until she would be Mrs. Kendall!

Gathering her things, she started to leave the room when she noticed Steve Carr had poked his head in the door.

"Can I talk to you for a minute?"

"Of course. Is this about *The Merchant of Venice*?"

"It's a pretty interesting story, but that's not why I'm here."

She rested her hip against one of the desks. "Have you been grounded again for something?"

"Not for a long time."

"I was kidding, Steve. What's wrong?"

"A bunch of the guys were talking in the cafeteria. I overheard them say something about the man you're going to marry, and I couldn't believe it."

She eyed him frankly. "If you're asking me if he's an ex-priest, then the answer is yes."

He studied her for a long time. "The man who came to class on back-to-school night? Whoa. He seemed cool."

"He is."

Through the junior ranger program she and Steve had grown to be good friends. "I can tell something else is on your mind. What is it?"

He hunched his shoulders. "Probably nothing."

"But you're not sure."

"Linda Smoot has been telling everybody he's going to go to hell for what he's done."

Sydney folded her arms.

"And there's more. She said her dad's going to get him fired, and your job's in trouble if you marry him."

What?

"I'm sorry, Sydney, but I thought you should know."

"Thanks for coming to me, Steve."

Furious over the gossip, Sydney whizzed home in her Jeep. Anxious to be on time for Jarod who was picking her up, she showered and changed into jeans and a ribbed, dark green sweater.

At first he was only a little late. But when it grew to be an hour and he hadn't come by the apartment or phoned, she got in her Jeep and drove over to AmeriCore headquarters to talk to him.

"Hi, Maureen."

The older woman at the computer nodded to Sydney. "I guess you heard."

Sydney walked over to her desk. "What's going on? One of my students told me something about Jarod's job being in trouble, but I dismissed it as rumor."

She eyed her compassionately. "I wish it were. He's in his office with the company attorney. I feel awful about this because I'm the one who hired him. My job's on the line, too."

"Why?"

"Several people on the board of AmeriCore here in Montana have decided that an ex-priest shouldn't have been allowed to fill the head counseling position."

"That's absurd! He's been doing it professionally for ten years! His credentials from Yale and the ministerial college in Minnesota are impeccable."

"That's exactly why I picked him for the job. His qualifications far exceed what was required."

"Who are the people on the board?"

"Among the most vocal are Tim Lockwood and Randall Smoot."

Now it was all making sense.

"His daughter, Linda, is in my English class. She's been spreading rumors at school."

"I'm not surprised. With his money and influence, he wields a lot of power."

What Maureen didn't know was that when it came to money, Jarod had the backing of the Kendall Mills fortune. If it was a matter of needing legal counsel, his brother Drew was a big New York City lawyer. Randall Smoot and his ilk would be way out of the Kendalls' league.

"Sydney?"

The second she heard Jarod's voice, she ran over to the conference room where he'd just emerged with a man of middle age.

"Darling? This is Jack Armstrong, the company attorney from Chicago. Jack, this is my fiancée Sydney Taylor."

"How do you do?" She shook hands with him. "I understand someone is trying to get Jarod removed from his job."

"I'm sorry to say it's true. Forgive me for keeping him this long, but it was necessary in order to prepare a preliminary report."

"I understand. If you need a character witness, I'm number one on a list at least 900 people long." That took up most of the town of Cannon.

The other man's mouth curved. "That's the way it should be. I'll see myself out, Jarod."

"Are you really in trouble?" she cried when he pulled her in the other room and shut the doors.

"First I need this—"

So saying, he swept Sydney into his arms. She sought blindly for his mouth, trying to infuse all the love, all the passion she felt for him in a kiss that would take away the sting.

"You make it all worth it," he confessed after relinquishing her lips.

She studied his features, looking for signs of distress. "Do they really have a case?"

"If a group of people decide to railroad you, and they get enough money behind them, then they have a case."

"Because you can't take this particular job if you've been an ex-priest? If that were true, Maureen wouldn't have hired you."

His lips twitched. "No. There wouldn't be

such a disclaimer. But if they decide that a man of the cloth who has broken his vows *isn't* the best role model to counsel other people in trouble, that's where the gray area comes in."

"Steve Carr spoke to me after class. He said the Smoot girl has been spreading rumors."

In an instant, his face became an impenetrable mask. His hands curled into fists. "We're not even married yet, and already your job is being jeopardized because of me."

She pressed a lingering kiss to his lips. "If you think I care one jot for what people think, then you don't know the real me."

To her immense relief, his body finally relaxed and they clung for a long time.

"I thought we had an appointment with the pastor."

"We did, but I changed it until tonight when I found out Jack was flying in. The hard part of this is realizing Maureen's job is on the line."

Sydney smiled up at him. "Because she showed how brilliant she was to have hired you?"

His expression grew solemn. "I love you, but I don't want my loving to cause you this kind of hurt."

"Didn't you hear anything I said? I'm not

hurt. I'm angry at people's bigotry. I always have been. It started in my own home where my parents couldn't see beyond the perimeter of their world.

"Of course I love home, but when I look back, I know the reason I ever entertained the thought of being a stewardess was so I could see what the world was like beyond the North Dakota prairie.

"I studied English literature in college because it broadened my understanding of people, fictional or real.

"Provincial types like the Smoots need to be confronted so they'll wake up and take a look at themselves instead of judging everyone else by their shallow, narrow standard of acceptance.

"It's sickening. Really sickening."

Jarod started to clap. He didn't stop until she was almost hysterical with laughter.

"I'm sorry. I didn't mean to go on and on like that."

He stole a deep, passionate kiss from her lips. "I wouldn't have missed that performance for anything. Let's go plan our wedding, shall we?"

She heard a whole new tone of happiness in his voice. It thrilled her.

"Yes."

With their arms around each other, they walked through the main office.

Jarod paused. "Good night, Maureen."

"Good night, you two. See you on Monday."

"I love your optimism, Maureen."

The older woman laughed so hard, Sydney could still hear it after they'd exited the main doors of the building.

CHAPTER EIGHT

ON TUESDAY OF the next week, Sydney had just walked in the door from school when her cell phone rang. Jarod always called her at this time of the afternoon. She lived for it.

"Hello?" she cried breathlessly, needing to hear his voice at the end of a grueling day. They always had so much to talk about. She didn't know how she'd survived the last year without him.

"*Aloooohhhhaaaaa.*"

"Gilly— You're back!"

"Yes!"

"I was expecting a call from you yesterday."

"We decided to stay another night. It was hard to come home, you know?"

"Yes. I *do* know." *Oh yes I do*.

"You sound different. Excited. I hardly recognized your voice when you answered."

"I hardly recognized yours," Sydney countered. "I don't need to ask if you're happy."

"There aren't words." Gilly's voice trembled.

"I know the feeling."

"Talk to me."

Sydney smiled. "How long have you got to listen?"

"Until my lord and master comes back."

"And you can't wait."

"I confess."

"Knowing how crazy he is about you, that won't be long, so I'll hurry and tell you everything."

"You've met a man while I've been gone."

"How did you know?"

"Because it takes a man to make you feel the way you sound. I can hear something new, even through the phone. After Jarod, I didn't thi—"

"It *is* Jarod."

The silence lasted so long, she knew Gilly was picking herself up off the floor.

Tears of joy filled her eyes. "He left the priesthood and came to see me ten days ago. We're getting married on Saturday at ten in the morning, in Ennis. We want you and Alex to be witnesses for us."

"*Sydney!*" her friend's ecstatic cry was deafening. "Do me a favor and start at the very beginning. Don't leave anything out. I want a blow-by blow-account."

Sydney had been dying for this moment. Gilly was the only person who'd lived through the fifteen months of heartache with her. Only Gilly, who'd lost her first husband Kenny, could have understood the kind of pain Sydney had gone through.

It was therapeutic to be able to confide in her best friend, especially with such joyous news. A whole world was going to open up now that she was going to be married, too. Sydney was so divinely happy, she could barely contain it.

"The first thing I did after you two left for Hawaii, was throw my maid of honor bouquet in the ocean. I decided to consign my love for Jarod to the sea."

"But the flowers came back."

"Yes! How did you know?"

"Remember that movie where Steve McQueen is trying to get off of Devil's Island? He figures out it's the seventh wave that escapes the undercurrent, so he counts seven waves before throwing in the coconuts that carry him out to sea?"

"I remember."

"Well, after that movie, Kenny and I tried the same thing, but found out there is no seventh wave in front of our house. Everything always comes back. I could have warned you and saved you the trouble."

Sydney laughed. "When I saw the roses strewn across the beach, I had this foreboding I was doomed forever. But everything changed the second I returned to Gardiner. After I'd driven to my apartment, Jarod was there!

"He'd been at the Park looking for me. Chief Archer had to be the one to tell him my new address. Oh Gilly—"

"Yes… I'm waiting…"

After ten minutes, Sydney came to the unhappy part. "I'm afraid none of our families are going to be there for the ceremony."

"Your parents just can't bring themselves to come?"

"No. I've phoned them to give them the date and time. Jarod has done the same with his family, but neither of us has had an answer back."

"That's horrible, but I know how much you love Jarod. And he's right. At thirty-eight, naturally he's anxious not to lose any more time, especially if he wants to be a father. Where are you going on your honeymoon?"

"We can't take a long one until Christmas. A beach vacation sounds marvelous to both of us, so I think we'll be going to Hawaii, too."

"Stay in Maui where we did. When I see you later in the week, I'll give you the brochures."

"That would be wonderful. I'll talk to you later then. I'm so glad you're home, even if *you're* not," Sydney teased.

"Of course we're happy to be back, but over there I didn't have to share him with a single soul, let alone a telephone. No emergencies."

That sounded like paradise to Sydney.

"Give Alex my best."

"I will. As for Jarod, I'm consumed with curiosity about that man. I honestly can't wait to meet him. Take care."

Sydney hung up, wondering why he hadn't called yet. Maybe she'd go over to his work and surprise him. It was almost time for their office to be closed for the day.

A hamburger and a movie would help her get through another evening while she waited to be with him day and night for the rest of their lives.

Maureen smiled when Sydney entered the main office. "He's still going strong in there."

"Is he alone?"

"No. He's in a session with someone. I don't expect he'll be much longer. Would you like a drink while you wait?"

"No, thank you." After a slight hesitation, "Have you heard anything about the case against you and Jarod?"

"There's going to be an unofficial hearing before the board in a couple of weeks. Don't let it worry you, and don't allow it to ruin your wedding plans."

"I won't."

"I don't think I've ever seen a man more excited to get married. I've been thinking all men ought to try being a priest for a few years first. It's just a hunch, but I think it would make them better husbands later." She chuckled.

Sydney couldn't help laughing, too. When it subsided she said, "So far Jarod's perfect."

"Is that right?" He spoke directly behind her.

She swung around. "I didn't know you were through—"

In his gray suit, his green eyes seemed to glow as they played over her features. He took in all the details that sent the blood rushing into her cheeks.

"My last appointment left through the other door of the office. So what else were you telling Maureen about me?"

"That's our secret," the older woman quipped. "Don't want you to get a swelled head too soon."

These days Jarod seemed to smile more and more. It had to be a sign that he was happy.

Her breath caught. "I came by to take you out for a change."

"I like the sound of that. Give me two minutes to make a phone call, and I'm all yours."

Since it was a warmer Autumn day than usual, they walked from his office to the drive-in holding hands.

Halfway there he kissed her cheek. "You don't know how many times I yearned to do this when we'd happen to meet on the street in Cannon."

"You mean when I managed to meet you, accidentally?"

"How many times did you lie in wait for me I didn't know about?"

"Every time."

Her confession must have shocked him because he stopped walking for a minute.

"You're serious."

"Yes. Now perhaps you understand the depth of my guilt. I knew your schedule, where you went to eat, the people you visited on a regular basis, the hours you worked at the farm and the hours you saw clients in your office.

"I tried not to take advantage of it all the time, but I spent those nine months plotting and scheming to make the most of every week where you were concerned. I'm sure you think less of me for doing that, that's part of the reason I left Cannon with every intention of never seeing you again."

He slid his arm around her shoulders before they continued walking. "Now that I think about it, you did seem to show up at the precise moment I was aching for you. It's a good thing you did. Otherwise I would have had to find more creative ways to make certain our paths crossed."

Impatient with herself she said, "Let's not talk about Cannon anymore. It's too painful. I can't relate to that period now. Tonight we're going to experience another first and go to a movie together. There's only one in town, so you have no choice over the selection."

His hand slid down her back to squeeze her

waist. "That's all right because in any case, I'll be watching you most of the time. I can't take my eyes off of you."

While she basked in his attention, they ate a quick dinner, then headed into the theater across the street.

"Gilly's back," she whispered once the film had started. "She brought some brochures in case we'd like to go to Maui for our honeymoon."

"Lovely as that sounds, how would you like to fly to Tahiti instead? There's a remote little island where I can get you all to myself."

His choice of words coupled by the intimate tone in his voice sent tingles of awareness through her nervous system.

"I wish it were Christmas right now."

"It'll be Christmas for me on a twenty-four basis once I can go to bed with you every night."

She let out an unconscious sigh. Their wedding was only a few days away now, but it seemed like a lifetime.

"I'm in agony, too." He read her mind. His thumb made circles against her palm. His touch was like liquid fire, dissolving her insides. By the time they left the theater to walk to their cars, the ache building inside her was close to unbearable.

When they reached the apartment and he'd walked her to the door, she linked her arms around his neck. "I haven't asked Gilly yet, but I thought it would be fun if she and Alex came for dinner tomorrow night. If you'll tell me your favorite food, I'll fix it." The last was whispered against his lips. She needed his kiss desperately.

In her amorous state, she was slow to pick up on the fact that he'd grown quiet and didn't exhibit the passion he would normally have shown. Something was holding him back. She lifted her head.

"What's wrong, darling?"

A pleading look had entered his eyes, as if he were hesitant to tell her what was on his mind.

"Have they moved up the date of that absurd hearing?"

"No. This is something else."

"If you're hurting because your family hasn't responded yet, don't let it ruin this time for us. Like you told me earlier, you haven't given up hope on them. In time they'll have to come around. How could they not?" she cried.

"This isn't about my family, Sydney." She heard him draw in a sharp breath. It alerted her that whatever was on his mind was so serious, he was afraid to tell her. That could only mean one thing…

Her mouth went dry. She eased out of his arms. "A-are you having second thoughts?"

"I knew you were going to ask that. It's a question I refuse to answer because you know the truth. But what I have to tell you is going to upset you." Tension palpitated between them. "The bishop has sent for me."

That did it all right. The bombshell she'd been dreading. They hadn't even taken their vows yet.

"When we were in my office earlier, I told you I had to make a phone call before we could leave. It was to return his call."

On a level of one to ten for pain, with ten being the highest, hers was a twenty. "Do you think the Pope has given permission for you to leave, and the bishop wants to tell you in person?" She was grasping at straws and he knew it.

That dreaded look of pity entered his eyes. She hated that look. He reached out to smooth some curls off her forehead. "No, Sydney. It's way too soon for that to happen, if it's ever going to."

"Could you ignore him then? I—I mean…legally? I mean, within the bounds of the Church?"

"I know what you meant," he whispered gently. "Of course I could ignore him. My business in Cannon is finished."

"But not your love for him or the Church—"

"No. That will never be finished. He's been a close friend for ten years. Naturally I couldn't turn him down."

"I know." She tried to smother her sob, but he heard it. His arms crushed her to him. Her face burrowed in his neck.

"Do you have any idea what this is about?"

"No."

"So it's as easy as that? He calls, and you come?" Her voice trembled. She hated herself for asking that question, but she couldn't help it.

"The bishop is probably the most understanding man I've ever met in my life. He wouldn't ask this of me if it weren't serious. I have to go."

She nodded, afraid to look at him once she'd backed away from him. Already she was finding out what it felt like to come in second-best.

The Church will always have a claim on him, her mother had prophesied.

"H-how much does he know about me?"

"Everything," Jarod answered solemnly.

"Even the kiss we shared?"

"Yes. He had to know it all."

She let out another cry. "He must despise me."

"No, Sydney. It's not in his nature."

Her heart raced like a runaway train traveling toward its doom. "You must have some idea of what he wants—"

His eyes grew bleak. "I could make a few guesses, but since he never uses the phone to discuss personal matters, I'm as much in the dark as you are. He's asked me to come as quickly as I can."

"How long will you have to be gone?" She couldn't bear it.

"I'm not sure, but you don't have to worry. I'll be back in time for our wedding."

"Does he know we're getting married?"

"I didn't tell him, but it's possible he's already talked to Rick."

"Then it's probable he wants to stop you before it's too late!"

"I can't answer for him. The only thing important here is that I'm marrying you on Saturday."

"Maybe, maybe not."

"*Sydney*—"

"I'm frightened, Jarod."

"I know you are. I wish I could take that fear away. You're going to have to trust me."

Her first test…

She tried to pull herself together. "When are you going to leave?"

"Right now."

Her pain was excruciating. "There aren't any flights to Bismarck this time of night."

"The Church has a plane for emergencies. He's sent it for me. There'll be a car waiting at the airport to take me to the rectory."

The bishop had sent a plane for him?

Her pain translated into borderline anger. She fought to control it. "If you knew about this before we went out for the evening, why didn't you tell me? We didn't have to go to that movie."

"Because I wanted to be with you tonight. I wouldn't have missed the evening you planned for anything."

"Don't you think I realize how important his call was to you?" she cried. "You could have caught a commercial flight earlier. If I'd known in time, I could have found a substitute for tomorrow and flown to Bismarck with you."

"Would you have gone to your parents to wait for me?"

"Probably not," she admitted. They'd hurt her too much by their silence.

"Then it's better for you to remain here rather than wait for me in an empty hotel room."

She couldn't fault his logic, but it hurt. It hurt so much.

He reached for her but she couldn't respond. "All this time tonight you've had the bishop's business on your mind," she muttered.

"No. You were the only person on my mind."

But not in your heart.

In order to live with Jarod, she had to share that space with his other love.

She tried to swallow. "I want to believe you."

"Then just do it."

Easier said than done.

"Could this be a matter of life and death? Do you think that's why he sent a plane for you?"

He eyed her with too much compassion. "I swear to you I don't know what this is about, but it sounds serious."

The fact that Jarod couldn't talk about it meant he was in terrible turmoil.

So was she. In a minute she was going to lose her dinner and the treats they'd eaten at the movie.

"Of course you have to go. I'm being exactly

the kind of person I don't want to be." Her voice wobbled.

"I'll find out what he wants and take the next flight back."

"What about your work?"

"On the way to the airport I'll leave instructions for Maureen on her voice mail."

Devastated by this unexpected turn of events, she unlocked her apartment door to keep distance between them. "You need to go. Don't let me keep you any longer."

"You're not keeping me, Sydney. I chose to be with you until the last moment."

It was the *until the last moment part* that was killing her.

"Have a good flight."

"Sydney—" His deep voice sounded gravelly.

"Please come back safely."

Please come back.

She shut the door, terrified of what all this could mean for the two of them.

Theologically, he was a priest forever.

"Tom?"

"Oh good, Jarod. You're here. Thank you for coming at such an unearthly hour. Come on in."

Jarod entered the bishop's private lounge. Only a few weeks ago he'd sat in this very room while they'd said their goodbyes. Being back here so soon was like déjà vu, except the intervening time with Sydney had changed him in ways that he was no longer the same person. Yet he couldn't deny the feeling of homecoming which was powerful.

The bishop sat down opposite him wearing a robe over his pajamas. No doubt he'd been asleep when the housekeeper had awakened him to tell him Jarod had arrived.

Tall and trim, he made an imposing figure, with or without his priestly vestments. He reminded Jarod a little of his own father, except that the bishop was warmer by nature and more open with everyone.

"I'm sure you're wondering why the call, and why the haste? For your information, Jeanine Adams, one of your parishioners, was hit by a car this afternoon on her way home from the high school."

Jeanine?

Jarod's eyes closed tightly. It was she who'd been instrumental in his finding out where Sydney had moved.

"Was she killed?" he whispered. The sight of her motherless three children flashed before his eyes. A deep despair washed over him.

"No, but if she recovers, she could be paralyzed."

He groaned in pain.

"It's my understanding that when she came to, she called for Father Kendall. Everyone wants and needs Father Kendall."

Jarod got to his feet.

"Like the rest of the parish, she's been told you're still on retreat. Father Lane has been with the family. Rick Olsen and his wife have organized some other families to take in meals and see about the children's care while her husband stays at her bedside."

Jarod covered his face. Talk about pain…

"It's devastating I know," Tom commiserated. "I also realize it's especially hard for you to hear bad news like this at this vulnerable point in your life."

Jarod stiffened.

Yes. *He was vulnerable.* He had self-doubts—fears that he couldn't live up to Sydney's expectations—concerns he might not be all things to her.

Did Tom believe Jarod was also vulnerable enough to consider returning to the priesthood?

Jeanine's accident was a monumental tragedy, something no one could have foreseen or imagined. But by sending for Jarod, Tom knew how the news would impact him.

The older priest had made it clear he was personally pained by Jarod's decision to leave. In his own way, Tom had treated him like he would a son if he'd had one.

Did he hope this horrific situation might pull Jarod back into the fold? He knew Jarod was conflicted, that a part of his heart remained with the priesthood.

His hands knotted into fists. "I'm no longer a priest. I can't go to her in that capacity now."

The bishop eyed him for a long time. "Maybe not now…"

Maybe not now?

Jarod had his answer. Tom still hadn't given up on him.

Sydney's fears were well founded.

Like a father who'd lost a son and yearned for him, Tom wanted him back in the society that had brought them together in the first place and had brought both of them so much joy.

He couldn't deny he missed that camaraderie known only by those who made up its ranks. The desire to rush to Jeanine's side and try to give what little comfort he could was almost overpowering.

But he could only be there for her as a friend, not as the priest who had the authority to bless her and use his office to pray with her. If he showed up at the hospital, it would be as a mere man, one who'd left the priesthood.

The shock of learning his changed status might do incalculable damage to her both emotionally and physically.

"God has given you this opportunity to rethink your decision, Jarod. With more contemplation and prayer, you could once again wear the mantle that has fit you so well. You're beloved to all who know you."

Kind as those words were, it was the bishop in Tom talking now.

"Have you been with Sydney Taylor?"

"Yes."

"I see. And what has come of your reunion?"

"We're being married on Saturday."

"So soon?" The older man sounded wounded.

"Yes. She's as anxious as I am to start our life together."

The older man sighed as if he carried the weight of the world on his shoulders. "Under the circumstances, I realize you won't like the question I'm going to ask, but out of my love for you, I have to ask it."

"Go ahead," Jarod said quietly.

"Even though you and Sydney have planned your wedding and are looking forward to it, does she truly mean more to you than one of your parishioners who's in dire need of the help only you can give?

"I'm not asking you to answer me. I'm urging you to search your soul one more time for the sake of your own ultimate happiness.

"Naturally having been with Sydney for the last little while, you have a whole new perspective on the decision that took you away from us. All I ask is that you stay here a few days and contemplate the enormity of what you're about to do.

"The housekeeper has made up a room for you, the same one you've used many times on your overnight visits. In the morning I'd like you to join me for breakfast and we'll talk some more."

Jarod nodded.

The older man's eyes misted. "I have to tell you it's good to see you again."

He cleared his throat. "I feel the same, Tom. Nothing's changed in that regard, and never will."

"Good. Now go to bed. You must be exhausted. If you're hungry, feel free to get what you want from the kitchen."

"Thank you. Good night."

The thought of food was insupportable to him. He went up to the room he'd slept in on other occasions and stretched out on top of the covers, cushioning the back of his head with the palms of his hands.

When he recalled the last time he'd been with Jeanine, tears trickled from the corners of his eyes.

Now she could be paralyzed.

A savage sound escaped his throat as his mind wandered over the rest of that red-letter day when Jeanine had managed to find Sydney.

He'd gone to a service station to make a phone call. While he waited for the outside phone to be free, he went inside to get a couple of dollars' worth of quarters. After the teens rode off on their bikes, he went back out and picked up the receiver, depositing two quarters.

The information operator connected him to

park headquarters in Wyoming and told him how much money to feed in the box.

He listened to the menu and pressed the digit that would give him a live voice.

It rang a long time. Finally he heard, "Yellowstone National Park." That had been the beginning of his journey down a different path.

Tonight Tom had asked him which woman needed him more. Where could Jarod do the most good?

For the rest of the night Jarod pondered that question. Interestingly enough, Tom hadn't asked what it was Jarod wanted.

The bishop in Tom knew instinctively which question to ask in order for Jarod to get the right answer. In so doing, it freed him from that dark angel he'd wrestled for so many months.

By the time the housekeeper rang to let him know breakfast was ready, the answer came to him with all the pure simple quiet of a beautiful spring morning.

When he arrived in the dining room, a lavish meal awaited him. It appeared the housekeeper had gone all out.

Tom was seated in his usual spot at the head of the table. "How did you sleep, Jarod?"

He sat down at his left side. "As you might imagine, I didn't get any."

The older man frowned. "I'm sorry."

"Did you really expect me to?"

"No," he said after an overly long moment. "That's what makes you such an exceptional man and priest."

"I'm not coming back, Tom."

"When you didn't knock on my door at five this morning, anxious to talk, I knew your answer. With hindsight I can see it was wrong of me to send for you and tell you about Jeanine."

Jarod shook his head. "I'm glad you did. During the night I had time to think. Just because I'm not a priest doesn't mean I can't go to her bedside as a friend. Before I rejoin Sydney, I'm going to drive to Cannon to see her. It's the least I can do. I'll let her husband decide if he thinks it's a good idea."

"You have my utmost admiration. I hope you'll always be my friend, too."

"You know better than to worry about that, Tom. Next to my father…" He couldn't get the rest of the words out. Rising from the chair he said, "As delicious as this breakfast looks, I can't eat. I hope you understand."

"Of course." The bishop stood up. "Feel free to take one of the cars. Just ask the secretary for the keys."

"Thank you."

"I'll always keep you in my prayers, Jarod."

CHAPTER NINE

JAROD LEFT THE dining room, fighting the unshed tears smarting his eyes. An hour later Rick met him outside the hospital in Cannon.

"Jeanine's doing a little better, Jarod. I'm glad the bishop called you. I debated telling you about her bec—"

"I know exactly why you didn't, but it's fine," he broke in. "My greatest concern right now is whether I should tell Brent the truth about myself before I walk in Jeanine's room."

His friend shook his head. "They'll both be so happy to see you, nothing else will be as important."

"Let's hope so."

As they started for the hospital doors, Jarod's cell phone rang, interrupting them. He checked the caller ID and clicked on.

"Sydney?"

"Jarod?"

The way she said his name sounded as emotional as he felt. "Is something wrong?"

"No. It's just that I thought you were going to call me this morning before class. When you didn't, I—I couldn't wait any longer to find out if you're all right."

He sucked in his breath. "I'm fine, but I'm afraid this isn't a good time to talk. I promise to phone you as soon as I can."

"Then I won't hold you up any longer."

"Sydney? Wait—"

But her line had gone dead before he could explain the precariousness of Jeanine's situation. With time of the essence…

Rick's eyes met his. "When you have a chance to explain the situation to Sydney, she'll understand."

"I don't know," Jarod muttered. He should have phoned her on the drive over to Cannon, but had decided to wait because he knew she was in class. There was so much to tell her, he hadn't wanted to leave it in a voice mail. "It's too late to undo the damage right now. Come on," he said to Rick.

They entered the hospital and found the room

where Brent was keeping a vigil at his wife's side. Though Brent's eyes widened at the sight of Jarod in a suit and tie, he didn't miss a heartbeat as he leaned toward his wife who lay there with her eyes closed.

"You have a visitor, honey. Someone you've been wanting to see."

"Father Kendall?"

He approached her other side. "It's Jarod Kendall now."

Her eyes fluttered open. "That's what I heard. Some-one saw you at the Bismarck airport with your fiancée."

"Yes. I've left the priesthood to marry a wonderful woman like you." He grasped her hand and squeezed gently. "Brent needs you the way I need Sydney, so you have to get better."

"I knew it," she murmured forcefully.

"Was I that transparent?"

"Afraid so. You should have seen your eyes when I told you where you could find her."

"Just don't despise me too much, or blame the Church for what I've done."

"Despise you?" she cried in surprise. "Don't you know you'll always be way up there in my estimation?"

"Thank you for that, Jeanine."

"I meant it. You're a remarkable human being. It's been my privilege to know you. Thanks for coming when I know you have other plans."

"Nothing's more important than visiting a friend. I hear your prognosis is excellent. That's a relief because I couldn't have given you the last rites."

Jeanine laughed gently. "Cannon won't be the same without the gorgeous Father Kendall."

"You must be feeling even better than I thought."

"I'll be up and around in no time. Don't be a stranger."

"Don't worry. I'll keep checking on you. Now you need to rest so I'm going to leave. God bless you."

"You, too. The woman you plan to marry is luckier than she knows. Tell her I said so."

There was so much he had to tell Sydney, he couldn't get home to her fast enough.

Rick walked him to the car. "Kay and I are looking forward to the wedding. We'll fly into Gardiner tomorrow afternoon. I'll call you when we reach the motel."

"That'll be perfect. We'll have dinner together."

His friend studied him briefly. "How did it go with the bishop?"

"Actually our visit was what I needed to lay my last demons to rest."

"Then I couldn't be happier for you. Be safe."

Sydney had told him the same thing.

On the way to Bismarck he called her, but naturally her voice mail was on because she was still in class. He left a brief message that he was on his way home to Gardiner and would call her later.

He supposed he could call the office and ask them if she could come to the phone. But unless it was next of kin calling, or an emergency, they'd probably tell him to leave a message. That wasn't good enough.

He needed to do something that would grab her attention. Something guaranteed to let her know she was on his mind…

As the germ of an idea took root, he called the information operator for Montana. By the time he'd reached the airport for his flight home, he was smiling in anticipation of her reaction.

By the time seventh period started, Sydney was in so much pain, she didn't know how she was going to make it through class.

She'd waited all night for a phone call from Jarod, hoping he'd break down because he couldn't stand to be apart from her and needed to hear her voice. Convinced he would phone her first thing this morning, she'd gotten ready for school early so she'd have time for a lengthy talk before first period.

But there'd been no phone call. She'd checked her messages between second and third period. Nothing.

That should have warned her not to bother him. When he'd answered his cell, he'd sounded far away and preoccupied, so totally unlike the man who'd given up the priesthood for her. His abruptness had left her devastated.

At this point she realized she couldn't lie to herself any longer. What was the expression? Whatever seemed too good to be true probably *was?*

Two weeks ago Jarod had appeared at her apartment without his collar like some magnificent apparition from a fantastic dream.

It was fantastic all right.

Things like that didn't happen in real life!

When he'd refused to move in with her, she should have seen through his clever smoke screen. What a twist of irony that when he'd arrived out of the blue, she'd thought he'd come to dally with her during his vacation from the parish.

Instead, he'd refused to touch her in order to make her believe he'd left the parish for good. She believed his story about his wanting to honor her by making her his wife before they went to bed together. Part of her had always doubted he would leave the priesthood forever and it seemed he had given up on her already.

No farce or tragedy Shakespeare had written could compare to the scenario Jarod had created. It was masterfully scripted and acted exactly like the play her class was working on right now.

"I'm still waiting for an answer, class. Let me repeat the question. Can any of you identify a folk tale woven into *The Merchant of Venice?*"

Several hands went up. "Amy?"

"It seems like in a lot of fairy tales there are always three wishes, or three tries at something. I was thinking that maybe the suitor having to choose one of the three chests to win his mate was like that."

"Excellent thinking, Amy. You're exactly

right." She looked around. "There's another folk tale, as well. Does anyone want to take a guess?"

Linda Smoot's hand shot up. Another irony that one of the men responsible for trying to drive Jarod out of Gardiner was this girl's father. It was the stuff that could have been lifted from the famous English bard's backlist of material.

"Go ahead, Linda."

"How about the way creditors make their victims pay. You see that all the time in stories about the Mafia."

Sydney nodded. "You've been doing your homework. Who can identify the greedy creditor? How about you, Randy?"

"Shylock."

"Correct." She looked around. "Steve? What undercurrent is stirred up when pitting a greedy Shylock against a noble Antonio?"

"They come from different faiths."

"That's right. Jew against Christian." *Priest against sinner*. "This next question is for anyone in the class. Does this theme have any relevance that you can see in today's world? If so, be prepared to cite a specific example."

Everyone in the class raised their hand. She was about to call on Mike Lawson when a garishly clad man holding a rectangular florist box under his arm entered the classroom from the back. His presence created a major stir.

It had to be some girl's birthday. Sydney had seen this kind of thing done before. At least the clown had chosen to come at the end of the period. There'd be no more discussion of the plot twist today.

The intruder looked around, playing the crowd. Everyone in the room had grown excited. "I've got a present here for someone. I'll give you a clue. The initials are S.A.T."

The kids laughed. Naturally. It was the name of the dreaded test they all had to take.

"What?" the man said. "No Susan in here? No Sam?"

"There's a Steve!"

"It's not my birthday, and my last name doesn't start with a T," Steve Carr said, red-faced.

"All right. Let's try another clue. This person once had a pony named Pickle."

The kids thought that was hilarious.

Sydney blinked. Pickle had been her pony when she was a little girl.

The flowers were for *her*. Sydney Anne Taylor. Her heart pounded outrageously. They had to be from Jarod, but she couldn't believe he re-membered those obscure little details about her.

She got up from the chair. "The bell's about to ring. Since the recipient doesn't seem to be in this class, if you'll leave the box with me, I'll check for a card inside and make certain it gets to the right person."

His thank-you coincided with the final bell of the day. She took the box from him. Everyone left the room except Steve. Sydney wished he'd gone out with the others, but she couldn't do anything about it now.

He grinned. "I bet I know who those are from."

"Let's find out, shall we?"

Her heart fluttering with excitement, she lifted off the top of the box.

What on earth?

He stared at her. "Don't you like them?"

"Yes, of course—" she blurted. But lilies were normally a funereal symbol. The end. To her mind they portended nothing good.

Then she saw the note.

With trembling fingers, she pulled the little card from its tiny envelope.

This short trip to Bismarck has been illuminat-

*ing. Just so you know before we see each other,
the path I've chosen is the right one. Jarod.*

She tried to smother her gasp so Steve
wouldn't notice.

*Was this Jarod's way of saying our love isn't
meant to be after all?*

Her pain went too deep for tears. She didn't
have any more to shed.

"Sydney? You look sick."

She shook her head. "I'm all right, Steve. It's
just that the person who sent these lilies doesn't
know I'm allergic to their cloying scent. Will
you do me a favor and take these to your mom
to enjoy? Just tell her no one claimed them, so
I let you kids draw straws and you won."

"You're sure?"

"Positive."

"Okay. You know that question you asked on
relevance?"

"Yes?"

"I felt like looking at Linda and telling her she
and her family had a lot in common with Shylock."

"For someone who didn't think they were going
to like Shakespeare, you're very astute. Tell your
parents you got A-plus in my class today."

"How about making that my permanent grade?"

"Maybe." She smiled at him. "See you tomorrow."

A few minutes later she left the building. Before starting up the car, she checked her cell phone. This time Jarod had left her a voice mail that he was on his way home.

There was no mention of anything personal. No mention of the flowers. He'd let the note say it all.

Were the lilies his way of softening her up before he had to face her in the flesh with the truth?

Sydney didn't want to hear it. In her frantic state of mind, she couldn't stand to go back to her apartment. If Gilly was home, she'd drive there.

Reaching for her phone to call her friend, she heard it ring and noticed it was Jarod calling again. Her heart raced with sickening speed.

Was he checking to find out if she'd received his gift yet? His consolation prize?

If I'd just met you first, Sydney.

She sat there afraid to pick up and listen to what he had to say because she feared her doubts had come true, and her mother's prediction.

That man could destroy you. I'm frightened for you, honey.

Terrified to find out he might be phoning to call off the wedding, she let it ring and headed straight for Old Faithful.

The plane had been delayed, putting Jarod down later than he'd planned. He left the Gardiner airport and headed for Sydney's apartment. Why didn't she answer her phone? He didn't know if she'd received his flowers or not.

His hands tightened on the steering wheel while he waited for the next light to turn green. That's when he saw a black-and-tan Jeep headed for Mammoth at top speed.

Sydney's?

He'd asked her to stay put at her place after school until he came for her. Deciding it couldn't be her car, he kept going toward her apartment. But when he arrived there, he couldn't see her Jeep. Completely frustrated, he made a check of the school grounds. Nothing.

Maybe it had been her car he'd seen after all. Why hadn't she gone home to wait for him? He phoned her again.

To his relief she finally picked up. "Hello?"

It didn't sound like her. "Sydney?"

"Yes?"

"Where are you? I've been trying to reach you."

"I've been busy since class."

That didn't sound like her, either. "Did you get my flowers?"

"Yes, I did."

He frowned. Something was wrong. "If it disturbed your class, I'm sorry."

"No. The period had come to an end. Your timing was perfect."

A groan came out of him.

He'd hurt her earlier this morning when she'd called and he hadn't been able to really talk to her. No floral offering could undo the damage. It was a mistake he would never make again, but how to convince her of that right now?

"Darling—"

"If you don't mind, I'm busy and can't talk to you. Maybe later?"

To his chagrin, she clicked off. Sydney wasn't behaving like the woman he knew and loved.

Though Gardiner was a small town, traffic was heavier this time of evening. With her head start, he'd have trouble catching up to her. Filled with a strange sense of foreboding, he called

Park information and asked to be connected to the chief of security.

After a minute, "Ranger Smith speaking."

"Larry? It's Jarod Kendall."

"Hello! How's the bridegroom-to-be holding up?"

"Not so well I'm afraid."

"Uh, oh. What's wrong?"

"I'm not sure, but I'll admit to you I'm worried. Ten minutes ago I thought I saw Sydney headed for Mammoth in her Jeep. We've had a slight misunderstanding."

He paused to clear his throat. "The truth is, something's wrong, Larry. I can feel it. If you or one of the rangers should happen to spot her, would you let me know? I'm on my way to the North Entrance right now to look for her. You can call me back on my cell."

"As soon as we hang up, I'll put out an alert. If she's in the Park, we'll find her. Just hold on."

"Thanks. I'm going to owe you for this one."

"It's what friends are for."

Jarod knew he'd liked Larry right off. Now he knew why.

Before she reached Norris, Sydney heard a siren. One of the patrol cars was after someone.

In a few seconds she realized that someone was herself!

What on earth?

She pulled to the side of the road and turned off the motor before jumping down from her Jeep.

It was a couple of the younger rangers out on patrol. She walked over to their truck as they were getting out. "What's up, guys?"

They both grinned. While one of them started talking on his cell phone, the other one said, "Hey, Sydney. Ranger Smith told us to be on the lookout for you. If we saw you, we should pull you over and detain you while we search your car."

"You're joking—"

"Nope. He was dead serious."

"Do the police have some hot tip that a couple of students hid a stash of drugs in my car somewhere?"

"I don't know. We're just obeying orders."

Frowning, she walked back to her car and opened the driver door. "Be my guest."

The two of them went over to her Jeep and did a thorough inspection. It was embarrassing to stand there while curious tourists slowed down as they drove by to find out what was going on. In a minute she noticed a blue car pull up behind the patrol truck and stop.

Jarod?

A wave of dizziness attacked her as he got out and started toward her on those long, powerful legs. His expression looked more forbidding than she'd ever seen it.

The rangers nodded to him before taking off in their truck. A few seconds passed before she realized they'd pulled her Jeep over for Jarod's sake.

"I don't know what you think you're playing at," he said with quiet savagery, "but I'd advise you to get in your car, turn it around, and head back to Gardiner."

She was trembling with pain. "How dare you involve Larry in this!"

"It's obvious you still don't know me well or you'd understand I would dare anything where you're concerned."

"Oh, I understand that all right—" She bristled with anger. "I found it out when those flowers came. Talk about *illumination*— But the gesture wasn't necessary."

His breathing had grown ragged. "I thought every woman loved roses."

"Roses—" she almost shouted at him. "You sent me lilies!"

He stared her down. "No. I sent you a dozen long stemmed hot-pink roses like the kind you threw in the surf. I wanted you to understand that you'll never get rid of me."

She spread her hands in a nervous gesture. "You honestly sent me roses?"

"All you have to do is call the florist and have them repeat back my order."

"But your note was with the lilies."

"Then that's their problem."

Oh, no.

She couldn't swallow very well. "I—I guess there was a mixup and someone else received your gift. Jarod, I—I don't know what to say."

"I don't want you to say anything," he ground out. "I want you to get in your car, or shall I pick you up and take you to your apartment in mine?"

Regardless of the audience passing by, he'd do it without a qualm and there weren't any rangers to protect her.

"No," she answered unsteadily. "I'll meet you there."

His eyes had turned so dark, no one would guess at their brilliant green color. While he watched her every move, she got back in the Jeep, but she was shaking so hard, she had difficulty putting it in gear.

Now that the understanding about the flowers had been cleared up, why was he so upset when she was the one dying inside? Didn't he know how much he'd hurt her by not phoning her from Bismarck in the first place?

The drive home passed in a blur of agony. He stayed right behind her. Every time she glanced in the rearview mirror, her eyes met the fiery accusation in his.

Surely he understood how difficult it had been for her knowing the bishop had sent for him under such mysterious circumstances just days before their wedding was supposed to take place.

Forcing air into her lungs, she pulled into her parking stall and jumped out of the car. Jarod closed in on her before she put her key in the lock of the apartment door.

Once inside, he closed and locked it, then folded his arms across his chest as if he needed to do something with his negative energy.

This was a side of Jarod totally foreign to her.

"Just tell me one thing, Sydney." He almost

hissed the words. "Why were you really running away from me? The truth!"

She tried to look everywhere except at him. "Because I didn't want to hear what you had to say."

He took a shuddering breath. "Even if the flowers were the wrong ones, I sent you a note that should have been self-explanatory. What in heaven's name went on in your mind to frighten you to the point you wouldn't answer my phone calls?

"If you'd listened to either of my messages, you would have known I was coming straight to your apartment from the airport."

Sydney wrung her hands. "You don't under-stand."

"Make me," he demanded, taking a step closer to her until she could scarcely breathe.

"When I didn't hear from you last night or this morning, I began to imagine all kinds of things."

"Go on."

She couldn't breathe. "Jarod—"

"Answer me."

"I was afraid you might not come back."

His jaw hardened. "You thought I was capable of doing that to you?"

She shook her head. "I didn't know."

"Our wedding is the day after tomorrow."

"But I didn't think there was going to be a wedding."

"Because you just assumed that once I was back in Bismarck, I'd change my mind about you?"

Sydney rubbed her palms against her hips nervously. "I feared the bishop's power over you."

He grimaced. "There's only one person who's ever had that kind of power over me. It's you, and you know it!"

"I guess I'm still having trouble believing it. When you got off the phone so fast this morning, I jumped to too many false conclusions."

His hand carved a furrow through his black hair. "That's why I sent the flowers. My visit with Tom put everything into perspective for me. I couldn't wait to come home to you so we could talk about it. But it wasn't something I wanted to discuss over the phone."

She drank in gulps of air, but it didn't help her breathless state. "I realize that now."

"You know what hurts? To watch you take off for the Park, hoping I wouldn't find you."

"It wasn't like that, Jarod. I was in so much pain, I decided to find Gilly and talk to her."

"*I'm* the person you're supposed to talk to." There was a bluish tinge around his mouth. "I'm going to be your husband. You're going to be my wife. We have no secrets. You have the right to call me anywhere, any time of the day or night, for whatever reason."

She bowed her head. "I realize that, but since you'd been on Ch-church business I—"

"Correction," he broke in. "I'm not a priest. I'm an ordinary man who was asked to come to the diocese by an old friend."

Sydney lifted her chin a fraction. "That's splitting hairs, Jarod. Please don't pretend about something this important."

His brows had become a black bar. "Who's pretending?"

"All right then. You're *not* pretending."

"Thank you."

He sounded so bitter.

"You honestly believed I went to see the bishop because I couldn't help myself? That I felt the clarion call to return to the life I almost gave up for a woman?"

She studied the ground for a minute before

throwing her head back. "Yes! When you didn't have the time to really talk to me, th-that's what I thought!"

His features hardened to steel. "Those roses I sent you meant that I was coming home to you permanently. They were my way of saying my love is for always and forever. For the rest of this life and the next.

"If you don't know it by now, then we have nothing, Sydney. You want to know why the bishop sent for me at the midnight hour? I'll tell you the truth.

"You were right about his motives. He wants me back in the fold. He saw an opportunity to make me reconsider my decision and used it to full advantage."

Sydney shot him an alarmed glance. "What opportunity?"

"The secretary who helped me search for you was hit by a car. They thought she was going to die. She asked for me. But when I got to the hospital, she'd taken a turn for the better."

"Oh thank heaven—"

"Jeanine's a wonderful friend, wife and mother. The bishop reminded me I had a whole parish of people like her who need me. Did the woman I love need me more?

"This morning I told him yes. You needed me more. You needed me so your life could be complete. I told him I needed you more, so mine would be complete. Neither of us would ever be fulfilled without the other.

"But it appears I was wrong about you. You don't need me enough to overcome your guilt, or your fear of losing me. I've given you all the truth I have in me, but it's not enough for you. I have a vision of spending my whole life trying to convince you.

"That's no life, Sydney. I'll phone the pastor and tell him I've called off our wedding. You can tell your friends what you want. I'll tell mine.

"Certain members of the board at AmeriCore want to get rid of me. Now they'll have their wish without putting me or Maureen through a needless, insufferable hearing."

He turned on his heel and in a few swift strides disappeared from the apartment.

She ran after him, calling his name, but he kept going. As he drove out of sight, she felt her entire world collapse.

CHAPTER TEN

"Dr. Haroldson?"

"Yes, Sydney. Come on in."

She shut the principal's office door and took a seat.

"How are liking your position by now?"

"The students are terrific, so are the teachers."

"But?"

"My life has fallen apart. My fiancé called off our wedding over a week ago. I thought I could handle it, but I can't."

"That's what personal leave is for. Why are you still here?"

"Because it's so soon after school has started to turn my classes over to a substitute."

"Your attitude is very commendable, but under the circumstances, do you feel you're giving the kids your very best right now?"

"No," she whispered. "That's why I came in."

"Since it's the weekend, it will give us time to find a substitute. Take all of next week off if you need it. Just give me a ring at some point and let me know how you're progressing."

"Thank you so much. I've left detailed lesson plans on my desk, and I've written other instructions on the board. The substitute shouldn't have any trouble following everything."

"If there is a problem, where can you be reached?"

"At my parents' in North Dakota." At least that was her plan for the moment. She couldn't think beyond it.

Jarod hadn't phoned or come near. He hadn't returned any of her phone calls begging his forgiveness. No doubt he was in Europe by now.

"I'll leave you their number and my cell phone number." She wrote everything down on a pad and handed him the slip. "Thank you for being so understanding."

He walked her to the door. "Let's hope your trip home brings you the solace you need."

It won't.

But Sydney couldn't stand her own company any longer, and Gilly didn't need a complication like Sydney when she and Alex were so happy.

After leaving school, she went home to pack and headed for the airport. She'd alerted her parents she was coming.

It was eleven at night when she reached the house in her rental car. Without worrying about her suitcase, she got out and hurried up the steps.

The porch door opened.

"Am I welcome?" she asked when she saw their faces in the aperture. "I don't mean for overnight. This afternoon I told the principal I needed time off. I didn't know where else to go but home where…I used to be happy."

Tears glistened in her parents' eyes.

"The more important question is, will you forgive us?" her mother asked. "We've talked of nothing but you and Jarod since you brought him home to meet us."

"Jarod's gone out of my life," she said woodenly. "You were right, and I was wrong, so let's not talk about forgiveness."

Her father put his arm around her. "We raised you the way our parents raised us. Mistakes have been made because we didn't want to see you hurt. But our little girl's hurting anyway, and that's our fault."

"No, it isn't, Dad." She wiped her eyes. "Jarod told me some things about myself I need to acknowledge and work on."

"It's time this family worked on things together," her mother declared. "We're going to do better. Come on in, honey. We're thankful you're home."

Her parents' attitude was so nurturing, it was the balm Sydney needed as she walked in the house.

"I saved dinner for you. All I have to do is warm it up, but if you're not hungry…"

"I'm not, but thanks anyway, Mom."

"Do you feel like talking, or do you just want to go to bed?"

"That's the trouble, Dad." She burst into tears. "With Jarod gone, nothing matters anymore. Not eating, not sleeping. He's my whole life, and I've lost him because of my pathetic lack of faith.

"All these years I've gone my own way without wanting any spiritual help, so it's my fault if I haven't developed into the kind of woman Jarod needs. He deserves someone who believes in his love without question.

"I've questioned everything, doubted everything. Who would want me for a wife?"

"Now you're being too hard on yourself," her mother asserted. "He's no ordinary man. Just knowing he's an ex-priest would cause any woman to be concerned that he might yearn for his old life one day. You can't blame yourself for that."

"But don't you see?" she cried. "I failed him at the first opportunity to show him I trusted him."

Her dad patted the sofa so she would sit down next to him. "Tell us what happened."

Sydney didn't need any encouragement to bear her soul. "So you see, he hates me now."

"I doubt that, honey. Any man who loved you enough to leave the priesthood couldn't possibly hate you. But with his pride involved, I imagine he needs time to cool off."

She blinked. "His pride?"

"Of course. It hurt him that you didn't believe in him. But that's because this is all so new to him."

"Your father's right, Sydney. He's used to people trusting him with their deepest secrets and fears. But you're not people. You're the woman he loves. That puts you in a special category.

"What you two need is time. After all, he came right from the parish to ask you to marry him. It isn't as if you had a long courtship."

"We had nine months—"

Her father shook his head. "That was no courtship. Neither of you knew anything except the most superficial things about each other. I'm not ruling out the strong physical attraction, but there's more to love than that."

"I know."

"You sound dead on your feet. I'll bring in your bags while you get ready for bed."

"Thanks."

She hugged both her parents before going to her old room. It wasn't until she was alone that she realized how kind they were being about Jarod. She'd been in so much pain, she was shocked to discover they could talk about him instead of closing up like they usually did.

If they'd been like this when she'd first brought him home...

No. It wouldn't have made any difference.

The fault for their breakup lay strictly at Sydney's feet.

Jarod hadn't let her parents' rigid attitude daunt him. In fact he'd urged her to give them time to come around. He had more faith and trust in people than anyone else she knew. Those were two of his special gifts.

Would that they could have been hers… Then she'd be with him tonight. They'd be married.

Gut-wrenching pain incapacitated her. When her father walked in with her suitcase, she was lying on top of the bed sobbing.

"Go ahead and cry, honey. Get it all out. It'll make you feel better. God gave us tears for a reason."

How many times had she heard that since she was a little girl? The tears had always seemed to work because she always did feel a little better after.

But not this time…

She was a grown woman acting like a child. It was time she grew up.

"Dad?" She slid off the bed. "It's really good to be home, but I'm going back to Gardiner in the morning. I've made a mess of everything so far, but it isn't fair to my students to leave them for a week because I can't handle my personal life."

Her father nodded. "When we're down, work's a wonderful panacea for what's ailing us. In time, things will get better."

They have to.

"I'll tell your mother."

Due to a delay in flight connections, Sydney didn't return to Gardiner until late afternoon the next day under an overcast sky. On the way to the apartment she picked up a few groceries before pulling into her stall.

A cold wind had sprung up. It disheveled her hair. There was going to be a storm. She shivered and hugged the sack next to her chest as she hurried inside the apartment with her suitcase.

But no sooner had she shut the door than she heard a knock. Assuming it was a neighbor, she set her things down in the foyer and turned to open it again.

A tall, superbly fit male dressed in jeans that molded his powerful thighs filled the aperture. His vibrant black hair brushed the collar of his blue denim shirt.

No.

It couldn't be.

It just couldn't be.

"*Jarod?*"

* * *

The wonder, the joy in her voice was something he would treasure for the rest of his days.

While he'd been waiting for her to react, he was afraid too much damage had been done. If she rejected him now, he didn't know how he was going to go on living.

But he didn't have to worry because in the next breath he was met by a golden-haired force that hurtled through space toward him. She would have sent him sprawling if he'd been a smaller man.

"I don't believe you're here—I thought you were in Europe and I'd never see you again—" she half sobbed her joy.

"I couldn't leave you," he confessed. "I've been in Ennis at a motel, licking my wounds, but I couldn't stay away any longer."

"Jarod, darling—"

At this point he was trembling as he buried his face in her hair. "You have to forgive me, Sydney. Can we start all over again?" he begged. "I need you. Without you the world's a wilderness and I'll be lost forever."

She lifted lavender-blue eyes to him. They almost blinded him with love light. "I'm the one who should be saying these things to you.

Forgive me for not looking into your soul deep enough to understand what you've been trying to tell me all along.

"I promise you I no longer feel guilty about my love for you. Our love happened to us pure and simply. I've accepted it because I know you're right about life being a journey. We never know whom we'll meet along the path.

"If you've chosen me to be your life's companion after all has been said and done, then I have to believe we're meant to be together."

His eyes glowed like hot green fires. "Today I came back to Gardiner and found out from your principal that you'd gone home to see your parents, so I called them."

"You talked to Mom and Dad?"

"Yes. I'm glad I did. They gave me their blessing to marry you. For a wedding present they've offered us the North Forty and the ranch house that sits on it. One day we can build our own house if that's what you want."

"Dad gave you the North Forty?" She was incredulous.

"Yes. The only thing they ask in return is that we get married at their house. They're hoping it'll be soon. How does that sound?"

"You *know* how that sounds."

She flung her body against him, hugging him so hard he couldn't breathe.

"I thought one day we'd start our garlic plant farm. Of course that's after you've finished your year of teaching school. It's something I always wanted to try, but there were too many other parish duties that took my time. I've done the research and know it will work."

"Of course it will!" She cupped his handsome face in her hands. "Anything you do works. You've won my parents over. I didn't think it was possible. I'm in awe of you, Jarod."

"Don't be in awe of me. Just keep on loving me."

Sydney already knew how to do that. In fact she had some definite plans of her own to show him the full depth and breadth of her love.

EPILOGUE

—

LOCALS CLAIMED North Dakota was experiencing the worst February weather in twenty years. A new blizzard had swept in across the plains, burying everything in its path.

The fierce sound of the wind created moaning sounds around the corners and eaves of the church. But Sydney wasn't concerned. This church where her parents had worshipped for the last thirty-five years had withstood similar whiteouts over time. It was still sturdy as a rock.

The rank and file members were no doubt curious about all the new faces assembled on this particular Sunday morning. A very pregnant Gilly and husband Alex had flown in from the Park along with Larry and his wife plus Chief Archer and Janice.

The six of them sat on the same pew with Rick and Kay.

On another pew Jarod's oldest high school friend, Matt Graham from Long Island, was there with his wife and three children, the oldest being twelve.

Earlier Jarod had ushered Sydney to the middle pew where she sat next to her parents. Her aunt Lydia's family flanked them.

Jarod handed her their precious six-weeks-old baby who was sound asleep before he walked to the back of the church to escort his family forward. His parents, his brother and sister and their families had all come.

Another story. Another miracle.

When Jarod finally sat down next to her he whispered, "Guess who else came, darling? They're seated on the back pew."

She craned her head to look around. "I don't know who you mean."

"Would you believe the bishop and Father Pyke?"

Her throat swelled with emotion. She pressed a soft kiss to his freshly shaved jaw. How many times had she done that since their marriage almost a year and a half ago?

How many times had they made love, rejoicing in the right to express their feelings in the most elemental of ways? Yet every time felt like the first time. Just looking at her gorgeous husband, let alone sitting next to him with their baby, made her breathless.

"They love you, Jarod. It's the greatest tribute I know that they would come to another church to honor you like this."

"Seventeen months ago I couldn't have imagined any of it."

"Neither could I." Her voice caught just as Pastor Gregson appeared at the front of the church to begin the service.

After welcoming everyone, especially the many visitors, his gaze fell on Jarod. "If you and Sydney will bring your baby forward please."

There was hushed silence as Jarod took the baby from her so she could get past everyone on the pew. Together they walked toward the pastor.

For a brief moment Sydney wondered if Jarod wished he were officiating at his own daughter's baptism. But when she dared a quick glance at him, she saw a face and eyes so full of love and tenderness for their child, she realized he had no other thought in his heart.

The pastor smiled at both of them before turning to the congregation. "As most of you know, the Kendall baby was born on Christmas morning. Such a wonderful gift deserves a special name.

"I baptize you Noel Taylor Kendall, in the name of the Father, the Son, and the Holy Ghost. Amen."

The ceremony didn't take long. When the pastor had finished, he said, "It's not customary for the father of the baby to speak, but in this case, I'm breaking with tradition because I have a feeling Jarod would like to say a few words on this most important day."

Pastor Gregson just went up miles in Sydney's estimation.

Jarod's hand almost crushed hers before he turned to face the congregation. She loved it that he had to clear his voice several times first.

"Sydney and I don't have the words to thank everyone here for coming. I thought I was happy on my wedding day." His gaze swerved to Sydney's. "But the arrival of Noel in our home has brought us infinite joy."

That's what he'd told her he'd been after. Ultimate, infinite joy.

"I know I could never have appreciated this moment the way I do if my life hadn't included my brothers who taught me the meaning of devotion and sacrifice.

"Before God, I pledge my devotion to my family, to my wife, to our daughter. Noel combines the best of the Taylor and Kendall families. She deserves the best that is in me and Sydney who's the love of my life."

Sydney bowed her head, too touched by his words to stay in control much longer.

Pastor Gregson smiled. "Lift the baby so everyone can see her."

Jarod raised their daughter high and showed her off like any proud father. A ripple of oohs and aahs resounded throughout the church interior.

With his hand around Sydney's waist, Jarod guided them back to the pew where Jarod's mother reached eagerly for Noel who was now wide awake after so much attention.

A baby.

What power it had to draw family together and help heal wounds.

As Sydney looked into her husband's moist green eyes, she realized he was thinking the same thing. When Noel was older, what a story her father would be able to tell her about his life's journey

"I love you, Mrs. Kendall," he whispered.

"Not as much as I love you, *Mr.* Kendall."

4 FREE

BOOKS AND A SURPRISE GIFT!

We would like to take this opportunity to thank you for reading this Mills & Boon® book by offering you the chance to take FOUR more specially selected titles from the Tender Romance™ series absolutely FREE! We're also making this offer to introduce you to the benefits of the Reader Service™—

- ★ **FREE home delivery**
- ★ **FREE gifts and competitions**
- ★ **FREE monthly Newsletter**
- ★ **Exclusive Reader Service offers**
- ★ **Books available before they're in the shops**

Accepting these FREE books and gift places you under no obligation to buy, you may cancel at any time, even after receiving your free shipment. Simply complete your details below and return the entire page to the address below. You don't even need a stamp!

YES! Please send me 4 free Tender Romance books and a surprise gift. I understand that unless you hear from me, I will receive 6 superb new titles every month for just £2.80 each, postage and packing free. I am under no obligation to purchase any books and may cancel my subscription at any time. The free books and gift will be mine to keep in any case.

N6ZED

Ms/Mrs/Miss/Mr ....Initials ....
BLOCK CAPITALS PLEASE

Surname ....

Address ....

....

....Postcode....................................

Send this whole page to:
UK: FREEPOST CN81, Croydon, CR9 3WZ